All's Fair In Love And Christmas

Jennifer Nice

First published in Great Britain in 2021 by
Write Into The Woods Publishing.

ISBN 978-1-912903-38-2

Cover design and typesetting by Write into the Woods.
Brushes used in cover from Brusheezy.com.

www.writeintothewoods.com
www.nicebycandlelight.co.uk

Other Books By
Jennifer Nice

Merry Christmas Eve Eve
That's It In A Nutcracker
All's Fair In Love And Christmas

The Idea Of You

Find them all at
www.nicebycandlelight.co.uk

One

Looking at the time had become less of a habit and more of a compulsion. Wendy had one hour to go before she had to leave the office to pick her children up from school. One hour. She could get a lot done in an hour. Then she'd leave the office and make her way back to her car, parked a short Tube ride away. After picking the children up, she'd make them something to eat and sort out her daughter's homework. Her son needed socks. She mustn't forget the socks. His Christmas bag still needed packing. Wendy always had to time packing his bag otherwise he'd empty it and wear everything just before going to his father's. The divorce had been the right thing to do but sometimes she remembered a simpler life when there weren't so many bags to pack. A couple of years ago, two weeks before Christmas, Wendy had been sitting in this chair, at this desk, contemplating Christmas presents and buying a tree. This year she was that woman who walked into the Tube station muttering, 'Socks,' under her breath.

She sighed and checked the clock.

Fifty-five minutes to go.

'Wendy? Can I have a moment?'

Wendy hid the jump of fright well, she thought. She smiled up at her boss and stood, following him into his office. She closed the door behind her and sat opposite him, his desk between them. There was always that moment of anxiety before he spoke. Why had she been summoned? Was this about the promotion? Was he about to promote her now?

'Are you all ready for Christmas?' Graham asked nonchalantly. He was around fifteen years her senior and while he would say his hair was pepper flecked with salt, it was definitely now more salt than pepper. His fingernails were short from where he bit them, something that had driven Wendy mad when she'd first joined the firm. Sitting in a meeting with a client next to a man who bit his nails had slowly become infuriating. It was a bad habit, he told her once, that had replaced the worse habit of smoking. After that, she didn't feel able to complain about it.

'Yes. Getting there,' she told him.

He nodded, tapping at the desk. The man always needed something to keep his hands busy. She watched distractedly. When was he going to get to the point?

'I think I'm actually going to have Christmas off this year.' Graham gave something of a laugh. 'We'll have filled the partner position by then, so I'm hoping we can all relax a little.'

Wendy nodded. Yes, the partner position. Is that why she was here? It was why she was here generally, in the building. It was why she'd taken this role. Just over ten years spent working cases, paying her dues, all so that she could make partner. This was going to be her year. It had to be.

'Claire's booked us a holiday. Which will be nice. Skiing. I can't stand it but I do like the idea of relaxing with a brandy surrounded by snowy mountains over Christmas.'

Wendy nodded again. Smile and nod, smile and nod, get on with it, man!

'The kids are happy but she left it late to book. It's been expensive.' Graham sighed. 'Do you have your kids this year?'

Wendy shook her head.

'With their father this year?' he continued before she could open her mouth. 'Divorce is a bitch. I should know, I was a divorce lawyer when I started out. Did I ever tell you that?'

Wendy nodded.

'You did,' she said. Multiple times, usually while a bit tipsy at the office Christmas party. He'd offered to help her when he'd heard about her divorce but she preferred to keep the whole thing out of the office.

'Do you have Christmas plans without them?'

'I'm going to my brother's,' said Wendy. 'He owns our old childhood home now—'

'Oh, that glorious old house out in the sticks?' Graham interrupted.

'Yes—'

'Wonderful. That sounds very festive. And relaxing, I hope? Does he have children?'

Wendy shook her head.

'No, he—'

'Nice and relaxing,' said Graham.

Wendy sighed inaudibly. Usually she'd put up a fight when Graham got into this state of cutting her off. Usually she'd call him on it, tell him to get on with it, tell him to let her get a word in. Usually she'd stick up for herself. This time, however, the words wouldn't come. Somewhere, in her head, that voice that usually broke forth at times like this was too exhausted to find the words. Her gaze drifted down to her black, flat shoes. They were more comfortable than heels but not as comfortable as trainers. She probably only had around thirty minutes left by now, once she got out of here she could swap the shoes for the trainers in her bag. As she shifted, her trouser leg lifted, showing off black sock underneath.

She had to pack her son's socks. Would he have enough? Of course he would, the boy hated wearing socks. Where did he get that from?

'Sue's off sick today, you know?' came Graham's voice.

'Hmm, I heard.' Wendy had fond memories of wearing thick, fluffy socks in winter, sitting by the open fire of the Manor. Her father would ask her if her feet were too hot, that she should move or take the socks off, but she never wanted to do either so she'd lie and say she was fine.

'Flu, she thinks. She'll be off the rest of the week, so we probably won't see her again until the New Year,' said Graham.

'Oh, that's a shame.' Sure, sitting with sweaty toes wasn't pleasant but her son was rarely sitting in front of a fire wearing thick, fluffy socks. Still, he always complained his feet were too hot. Were her feet always too hot? She wiggled her toes in her shoes.

'Which rather throws the Christmas fair into a dilemma,' said Graham. 'She was organising it with one of our juniors. He kindly volunteered to help.'

Her toes didn't feel hot. The action of wiggling them reminded her of being warm, in bed. A wave of exhaustion washed over her.

'And, of course, we can't cancel the fair. It's on in a week and so important to our reputation. The marketing team have already done the PR. All those people we don't want to disappoint.'

He must get it from his father, Wendy decided. Her ex-husband had always had hot feet in bed. She'd loved it when they'd first gotten together. For a while there, right at the beginning, he'd let her warm her cold feet on him during the winter nights. Something in Wendy's chest ached.

'So, we need a new volunteer to organise the Christmas fair and I realised I know just the person. You, Wendy. So, I'll introduce you to James and you can get acquainted. Yes?'

There was a pause. A silence that filled the room and infiltrated Wendy's thoughts. She blinked and looked up.

'Sorry?'

'You'll finish organising the Christmas fair with James,' said Graham.

Wendy was certain there was a question mark missing.

'I have a pretty heavy caseload at the moment, Graham.'

'Sue's already done most of the organising. It won't take you much time. And there's only a week to go. It'll be over before you know it. And you said you're ready for Christmas, kids aren't with you, so less to prepare, right?'

'That's not really—'

'The Christmas fair is on Friday afternoon. We're making our final decision about who becomes partner at the end of Friday. Right before we close for the year. So once the fair is over, you can go home, grab your bags and head to your brother's. What a great way to finish the year.'

Wendy hesitated, her tired mind desperately trying to work out why he'd slipped in the part about the promotion.

'Graham.'

'I've already checked your cases. Nothing's closing this week. You should be fine.'

'Graham, does my organising this fair have any impact on whether I get the promotion?'

Another pause, this one heavier than the last as Graham's eyes lifted to meet hers.

'Of course not,' he told her. 'We couldn't do that.'

Wendy let the silence fill the room until Graham smiled.

'I'll introduce you to James now, shall I?'

She blinked.

'James?'

'The junior who'll be helping you. He was helping Sue. He'll catch you up and you can delegate to him. See, I told you it'd be easy.'

'Graham—'

He was already up, walking towards the door and beckoning for Wendy to follow. Once out in the main open office, she could hardly raise her voice and make accusations, so she followed silently. This was an opportunity to gather her thoughts, which is why her eyes were down and she nearly bumped into Graham when he stopped.

'James, this is Wendy Winshaw—'

'Hargreaves.'

'Hmm?'

'I've reverted to my maiden name,' said Wendy, still trying to corral some logical, sensible thoughts.

'Right. This is Wendy Hargreaves, one of our senior associates. She'll be taking over from Sue. I want you to catch her up and help her in any way you can. Let's make this fair a great one.' Graham grinned at them both.

Wendy finally lifted her gaze, looking from Graham to this junior called James. He wasn't what she'd been expecting. When she'd heard "junior" she'd conjured up a mental image of a young person, perhaps in their early twenties, straight out of university. This man could pass for late twenties but there was something about him that screamed thirties. Something grown up, something more mature, a certain look about his dark eyes. While the other juniors wore suit jackets, James had removed his and rolled his sleeves up. His arms were muscular and covered with thick, dark hair. That was not something Wendy should have been noticing. She looked back up into those dark eyes and he smiled at her, holding out a hand.

'Pleasure to be working with you,' he said in a smooth voice. He was clean shaven but the afternoon was becoming late and stubble was already making its way back to his chin. He smelled of coffee but there was still a whiff of cologne or aftershave about him.

'And you,' said Wendy, all rational, logical thoughts so carefully processed on the walk over were forgotten. She shook his hand and he gave hers a small squeeze that twisted her stomach. She tried to blink the feelings away.

'Excellent,' said Graham. 'I'll leave you two to it.'

Wendy opened her mouth to protest but Graham had already left, finding someone to drag with him in a loud conversation so she couldn't call him back.

'You sod,' she muttered.

'What's that?'

Wendy turned back to James and attempted a smile.

'Nothing. Nothing.'

'Okay.' James cleared his throat, looking away. 'Do you want to go through the fair plans now?' He looked back to his desk.

Wendy pulled her phone from her pocket and checked the time. She sighed.

'Sorry, I have to dash. Can we do it first thing tomorrow? When do you get in?'

'Eight.'

Wendy blinked. Eight in the morning. She remembered what she used to be able to get into the office at eight in the morning. In the days before the children. In the days before the husband, even.

'Okay, half nine?' she asked. 'Let's get together and go through it then.'

James nodded.

'Sure. Half nine tomorrow.'

There was an awkward pause as James sank back into his chair and Wendy realised she was standing there for no good reason.

'Right. Great. Thanks. See you then.' She swiftly turned on her heel and marched away, her chest and cheeks burning. She wiggled her toes as she walked and there it was, a bit of sweat. She almost laughed. As if she had time right now for butterflies in her stomach and staring at men who might possibly be quite attractive. Christmas was in just over a week, her workload had potentially just doubled and she still had to pack her son's socks.

Wendy had been dressed in one of her many smart suits, navy blue with a stylish red jacket, and ready for forty-five minutes but that didn't mean they were close to leaving the house that morning. She folded her nine-year-old son's clothes and placed them gently in a bag while he argued with her.

'I don't want to wear socks today.'

'You'll get cold feet,' Wendy told him.

'No I won't.'

'It's December, Oliver. And you only have one more week of school left.'

'So, one more week of wearing socks?'

'I tell you what,' said Wendy. 'You can take your socks off as soon as you get home, if you like. See how long your feet stay warm, yeah?'

Oliver gave this some thought and while he did, Wendy congratulated herself on not suggesting that her son only wear socks until he was with his father for Christmas. Their divorce wasn't one of petty squabbles or game playing, as tempting as it was at times. That had been one of her rules when they'd decided to break up. They had to remain kind to one another, thoughtful and friendly, even when they really didn't want to. Even when they were hurting. It was a year since the divorce had come through and, while the pain was still somewhat there, the kindness had become a habit.

'We're going to be late!' shouted Emma from the front door.

Wendy exhaled in a whistle through her teeth. If she had a pound coin for every time her twelve-year-old shouted through the house she could quit her job. That thought caught her by surprise.

'Mum? Are you okay?'

Wendy blinked and found herself frozen, bag half zipped up. She shook herself awake.

'Yes. Yes. Your bag is almost packed, so I'll put it under your bed for now. Okay? Don't take anything out of it but you can add anything you want to take to your dad's. Yeah? Got your socks on?'

Oliver wiggled his socked toes at her.

'Good. Shoes. Quickly now or we'll be late and Emma'll shout at you.'

Oliver pulled a face and ran off to find his shoes. Wendy took a final glance around her son's bedroom and then closed the door, following him down the stairs.

Emma was waiting by the front door dressed in her school uniform, her soft brown hair, inherited from Wendy, tied back in a high ponytail. Wendy hesitated on the stairs long enough to think for the umpteenth time just how much her daughter took after her. Sometimes she wasn't sure that was such a good thing but when it came to school, it was wonderful. As long as Emma stayed on track and wasn't dissuaded by hormones, she would likely follow in her mother's career footsteps too.

For the first time upon having that thought, Wendy frowned. Her hand went to her stomach as it churned.

'Mum?'

Wendy looked up at her daughter.

'Yes. I know, we're going to be late. Come on, Olly!'

Wendy slipped on her trainers, grabbed her bag and car

9

keys, scooped an arm behind Oliver to hurry him out of the house and then locked the door behind them all. Once in the car, Wendy began the drive to the primary school first. In the back, Oliver stared out of the window while in the front passenger seat, Emma studied her phone. Radio turned up, Wendy tuned out.

She would drop the kids off at school then make her way to the car park. She'd stand on the Tube into central London, grabbing a coffee on the way, and reach the office with time to spare. Just like always. She had a few pieces of work to do and some emails to send before she met with James. It would be good to go into the meeting with a clear head.

As far as she was concerned, most of the work was already done. So she could just approve the plans already in place, tell James to put them into action and then get back to her proper job. Except, of course, if the plans were bad because now that would reflect poorly on her. Or if the plans were incomplete. Or if James couldn't put them into action. Or—

'Mum?'

'Hmm?' Wendy pulled over near the primary school.

'Can I go round Stevie's tonight?' Emma asked, exasperated. How many times had she asked while Wendy wasn't listening? No, she was already acting like a teenager, she'd probably only asked the once. The whine in Emma's voice was becoming a permanent thing, something she was learning from Stevie, Wendy suspected. That girl had started whining at the age of eight when her sister had entered her teens. It was enough to give Wendy an eye twitch.

'Do Stevie's parents know?'

She could feel her daughter rolling her eyes.

'Yes. Otherwise she wouldn't have asked.'

Wendy sighed.

'Home by six,' she told her and then held up a hand to silence the protests before they could leave Emma's mouth. 'You have homework to do, school tomorrow and you need to finish packing for going to your dad's.'

'I've still got a week to do that,' said Emma.

'Yes but remember last time? You ended up wearing that top you wanted to take and it was right at the bottom of the washing basket? We don't want that happening again.'

When Emma didn't respond, Wendy risked a glance from the corner of her eye. Her daughter's lips were twisted in an angry pout. Wendy forced away a smile. Emma wanted to argue but there was no logical argument to make, and her daughter was nothing if not logical in her arguments.

'Are you going straight from school?' she asked, only to break the silence.

'Yeah.'

'Okay. Message me.'

'Yes, Mum.'

Wendy ignored the tone. It was only there because Emma was angry she'd lost the argument. She checked Oliver in her rear view mirror.

'You don't have any invites for after school, do you Olly?'

'Nope.'

'Okay.' It might have been nice to not have to worry about getting home so early for them, it would have given her some breathing space. But she'd learnt long ago that after school friend visits couldn't be forced. She got Oliver out of the car, kissed him on the cheek and watched him walk into the playground and into school, waving when she thought he might look back. He didn't. Sighing, she got back in the car. The radio played Christmas music as she drove to the secondary school. It was so close to Christmas. Wendy just had to push through this last unexpected hurdle. Emma climbed out of the car after a brief hug, where her friends wouldn't see, and Wendy was alone. She turned up the radio and started singing along, as loud as she could, until her throat ached and she reached the car park.

Wendy strode into the office bang on time. She settled herself, making a fresh coffee, and checked through her emails. Something – although she couldn't for the life of her say what it was – made her look up just as James walked through the office and past her desk. He was looking down at his phone, coffee in his hand, and a waft of London mixed with cologne came off him as he passed. Wendy stayed looking at him, waiting for his eyes to meet hers so she could tell him they'd talk later, but he didn't look up. He walked past and away, disappearing into a different part of the office. Wendy blinked, her hand finding her stomach. It had to be anxiety about the stupid Christmas fair, she thought. She went to pick up her coffee but thought better of it and sipped at her water in an attempt to calm the fluttering.

'They won't let me have my tinsel.'

Wendy jumped and peered up at the woman next to her.

'What do you mean, they won't let you?'

Kit, a petite, brown-haired woman who looked seventeen but was forty-six (Wendy had been at her last birthday party and had pried the number from Kit after too many gin and tonics), did a flounce as she sat in her chair at the desk beside Wendy.

'Apparently it's distasteful and a fire hazard. Well, it wasn't distasteful and a fire hazard last year. Do you think it's distasteful?'

Wendy studied her friend. They'd met on Kit's first day at the firm when Graham had seated her next to Wendy and told Wendy to show her the ropes. The ropes, on that day, had involved a lengthy tour of the best local restaurant for lunch where the two had discovered a passion for Christmas in common, among other things.

'That depends. What colour was it going to be this year?'

'Silver.'

'That sounds very tasteful. It is a fire hazard, though. And they're hotter on that this year.'

Kit exhaled sharply.

'Health and safety gone mad.'

Wendy slowly turned to look at her friend. Kit grinned and together they whispered under their breath, 'Elf and safety,' before erupting into giggles.

Wendy pulled herself together, sipping at her coffee.

'What did Graham want yesterday?' Kit asked.

'Oh, Sue's gone off sick so I'm to finish organising the Christmas fair.'

This time Kit turned slowly to look at Wendy.

'What? You? Why? How?' She gestured at Wendy's desk and the piles of electronic work that were symbolically stacked upon it.

Wendy leaned over the gap between them so she could lower her voice.

'Not a clue. But they're making the decision about who becomes partner afterwards.'

Kit's eyes widened as the realisation hit her.

'So, you'll only make partner if you can pull off the Christmas fair?' she hissed, shaking her head as Wendy shrugged. 'That's not legal.'

'That's why it's not official.' Wendy sat back. 'I'm guessing. I mean. Maybe I got the wrong end of the stick.' She held up her hands to proclaim innocence.

Kit studied her for a moment.

'What're you going to do?'

Wendy sighed. That was the big question. The one she'd been avoiding all evening. The one she daren't ask herself. She shrugged.

'Get on with it, I guess.'

Kit emitted a soft growl.

'It isn't right. Who's taken over from Sue while she's off? Why can't her team handle it?'

'Look, I'm sure I'm blowing it all out of proportion. Graham says Sue has already organised the thing. I just need to see it through and I'll have the guy who was assisting Sue to help. I'm sure it'll be fine.'

Kit didn't look as sure as Wendy sounded.

'What guy?'

'James something-or-other. One of our juniors.'

Kit's brow furrowed as she tried to place the name.

'Is he cute?'

Wendy shot her a warning look. Kit shrugged.

'Just saying. Something good could come from all this.'

'Yeah, like me being promoted.'

'Oh, I meant before that. It is Christmas, after all.' Kit gave a dirty laugh that Wendy could never resist. She smiled to herself.

'Doesn't your brother's girlfriend organise Christmas events? Maybe she could help,' Kit suggested after a moment of silence as they went through their inboxes.

'Yup. Eve. She's now his wife and they're currently on honeymoon.'

'In December?'

'They were going to have a Christmas wedding but they've started a tradition of holding a Christmas ghost tour in their house in my father's memory. He loved holding ghost tours there and Eve always organised them. They now do a ghost tour before Christmas and a Christmas fair. The fair was at the beginning of the month this year, then they got married, and they'll be home in time for the Christmas ghost tour.'

'Cor. She sounds as married to her job as you are.'

Wendy didn't respond to that. Her gaze drifted down from her computer screen to a photo of her children, wedged between her pen pot and coaster.

'She loves Christmas,' she murmured eventually.

'Is that your whole family, then? A load of Christmas lovers?' Kit asked, tapping away at her keyboard.

Wendy smiled.

'My older brother's with a professional baker,' she said. 'Beth makes a mean gingerbread man.'

Kit laughed.

'And yet you never bring anything into the office?'

'I meant to last year, but I ate it all instead.'

The two women glanced at one another before giggling quietly. They were interrupted by Kit's phone ringing.

Wendy turned back to her work. Her emails were organised. Sure, there were a couple of calls to make but they could wait. She wondered if James was available now. She typed out a quick message to him and hit send. A reply popped up as she sipped her coffee. He was ready when she was.

Three

Wendy exhaled slowly as she wandered over to the meeting room she'd booked for her and James. Her laptop was under one arm and her free hand held a full cup of coffee. He was already in there waiting for her. When she saw him through the glass wall, she slowed. His head was down as he studied his phone. Was he checking social media? His laptop was in front of him so he wasn't looking at emails. Perhaps his wife had messaged him. Or his girlfriend. Or boyfriend, or husband... Wendy mentally shook herself. What did it matter if a partner had messaged him? His shirt sleeves were down this morning but her eyes were still drawn to his arms and his fingers, sliding over the screen of his phone.

'Crying out loud,' Wendy muttered to herself, silently banishing any butterflies that were threatening to fall into her stomach. She pushed open the door and almost dropped her laptop on the large table in the centre of the small room.

'Good morning,' she said a little too briskly.

'Morning.' He looked up, placing his phone screen down on the table.

Wendy arranged herself, opening her laptop and sipping her coffee. He'd brought a glass of water, she noticed, which sat untouched.

'Everything okay?' she asked as her laptop woke up. James nodded, studying his own laptop screen as he tapped some keys.

'How did you get roped into helping Sue organise this, then?' Wendy asked, unwittingly tapping her foot as the unnecessary nervous butterflies were pushed from her stomach and into her toes.

A small smile flittered across James's face but he kept his eyes on his screen.

'I volunteered. For some reason I thought it would look good.'

Wendy smiled to herself.

'Apparently it does look good,' she murmured.

James looked up at that.

'Does it?'

She lifted her gaze automatically and locked eyes with him. His were a deep brown, as dark as the hair on his arms, and then the butterflies were out of her toes and back in her stomach, tapping their wings against her insides.

'That's why I'm here,' she said weakly.

He gave her a curious look and Wendy cleared her throat.

'So, the fair is in a week. I imagine Sue has everything sorted by now?'

James laughed. It echoed around the minimalist room, making Wendy jump.

'She should have done but nope.'

Nope. Wendy blinked.

'What do you mean, nope?'

James's shoulders sagged and he turned his laptop so the screen faced her.

'This is the folder we shared with everything in it. This is a list of all her ideas. This is a spreadsheet of everything that needs doing.' He opened the document. 'See this column? This is the completed column.'

There was a long list of things to be done but the completed column was gut-wrenchingly empty. Wendy pulled her gaze from the empty spreadsheet column to the one filled with the to do list.

Book stallholders.
Contact charities.
Create layout and map.
Organise music.
Organise food.

She looked up at James, eyes wide.

'Tell me most of this is done and she just forgot to tick it off,' she murmured in a hushed voice, terrified of the answer.

James's eyes softened and he slowly shook his head.

'But…but the stallholders are booked. Right?'

'Some are,' said James. 'But not enough. Maybe three?'

'Three! Okay. But the charities are sorted, right?'

'Oh, yes…sort of.'

'Sort of?'

'Well, Marketing sorted most of it and I think Sue had some initial chats. We have our main charity but it was originally decided we'd work with three. We could change that, though, I guess.'

Wendy sighed. The space between her eyes twinged with the makings of a headache.

'How has this happened?' she murmured, thoughts spinning. 'No, okay, if we have to do this right then we'll need the three charities.' She refrained from swearing.

James sat back in thought.

'Two small charities. What's your favourite one?' Wendy asked.

'A local one that helps homeless people with their pets,' said James.

Wendy smiled, glancing up at him.

'Mine's a homeless charity too but focusing on the people. Great, we'll approach them.' Wendy scribbled down the note. 'You contact yours, I'll contact mine. Tell them the proceeds will be split into thirds. Is that what Sue had planned?'

'Think so,' said James, making a note for himself.

Wendy nodded. One thing down, many more to go. Arguably, choosing charities was the easy part. She sighed, staring at the to do list. What was next? Her chest was tightening with each breath. How was she going to pull this off? They had one week, nothing was planned, and she was a solicitor not an event organiser. Even an event organiser couldn't pull this one off.

'At least the venue's booked,' she murmured.

The silence made her look up at James. He was cringing. 'That's also a nope.'

'What?' Wendy screeched. 'There's no venue? There's no venue.' She sat back as it sank in. 'How the hell are we going to do this in a week without a venue? Everywhere'll be booked. Why hadn't Sue done anything? Why hadn't she at least booked a venue?'

'She hadn't been feeling well for a while,' James told her. 'She reckons she was burned out. I reckon she…well, that's not important.'

'No, go on.' Wendy leaned forward so they could lower their voices. 'You reckon…' she urged.

James glanced around as if there might be a spy sitting in the corner of the meeting room and then leaned closer, whispering, 'I reckon she's not ill. I reckon she's bailed because she didn't book a venue.'

'But why?' Wendy asked. 'What were you doing through all this? Couldn't you have booked a venue for her?'

James stiffened and sighed, shoulders heaving.

'I tried, believe me. I kept offering to do things. I told her so many times I was happy to book anything and everything and she kept saying, over and over, no, she had it under control. Until one day I told her that it was okay if she was struggling or whatever, that's what I'm here for, to help. I said I'd go book a venue that minute and she pretty much screamed at me not to. I have no idea what was going on with her, but I doubt she's really ill. And I wanted to help. I'll do whatever you want me to, but c'mon. I'm the new guy here. I've never done this before. I didn't want to overstep my bounds and suddenly this woman is screaming at me not to do anything. So I didn't.' James slumped back in his chair.

Wendy watched, her foot tapping faster against the floor.

'I'm sorry she shouted at you. That's not on at all.' What had Sue been playing at? Wendy didn't like to think badly of the woman. She'd organised the Christmas fair before, although Wendy couldn't remember how good it had been. Had she even attended? Maybe Sue was just overworked, overburdened, burned out.

Wendy stifled something of a hysterical laugh, thinking of the stacks of cases, the clients who had burst into tears during their meetings, the running from work to school to home, the worry, the sleepless nights wondering what she'd forgotten. Running a hand over her face, Wendy shook her head.

'This is insane. I can't do this.' She hadn't meant to say that last bit out loud but there it was, hanging over the table between them. She daren't look up at James. That was certainly not something a senior associate was supposed to say in front of a junior.

He didn't say anything. Why wasn't he saying anything?

She risked a glance at him. He was staring down at the table, lips pursed, possibly thinking through his options. That's what she should have been doing.

'I'll talk to Graham,' she murmured after a moment. There were only two options: get on with it or talk to Graham. Her first move was obvious. 'Can you give me access to that to do list?'

James nodded, pulling his laptop closer. Wendy moved to stand.

'I'll let you know what happens.'

'What about the charities?' James asked, following her.

'If we don't hold the fair, I'm sure the firm can still donate,' said Wendy, heading for the door. She had to catch Graham quickly and hope that he was in a good mood. Surely he'd see the sense of cancelling the fair. He had to.

'Thanks,' she added as she left James by his desk.

There was a part of her desperate to turn around as she walked away, to give him a reassuring smile perhaps, which was ridiculous.

'Focus,' she muttered as she spotted Graham heading into his office with a fresh cup of coffee. 'Graham!' she called, breaking into a light mince of a jog which was arguably no faster than the walk she'd been doing. It did the trick, though. He hesitated to look at her, his brow creasing in tired curiosity.

'Everything all right?' he asked as she reached him.

'Do you have a moment? I need to talk to you,' she said, heaving her laptop under her arm and hoping she'd be able to find the spreadsheet easily.

Graham gestured for her to enter his office and he closed the door behind them. Wendy took the chair opposite his desk and opened her laptop. An email from James pinged through with a link to the spreadsheet. She exhaled in a rush.

'What's this about, Wendy?' Graham sat in his chair, sipping his coffee.

'I just met with James about the Christmas fair,' said Wendy, head down, eyes still on the screen as she pulled up the document. 'He showed me how much Sue has done so far.'

'Hmm?'

Wendy lifted her laptop and turned it, placing it on the desk so Graham could see the to do list with nothing completed.

'She's done nothing, Graham. Nothing's done. Nothing's ready. There's not even a venue booked. What the hell was she doing in all that time? James kept trying to organise it for her and she kept telling him no until she shouted at him. She shouted at him, Graham. He did everything he could and she did nothing. Now we have one week to pull off this huge event. It's not possible.'

There was a silence as Wendy waited, heart pounding. Graham's eyes flicked over the screen. Then he leaned forward and pulled Wendy's laptop closer, working his way through the document, his features dropping until finally he heaved a deep sigh.

He sat back in his chair, staring through Wendy, biting his lip in thought, tapping his fingers against the desk. She watched and waited, her mouth dry.

'Last year you mentioned you had invested in your sister's business,' Graham said quietly.

Wendy's heart fluttered. That wasn't the reaction she'd been expecting.

'Well, yes, my sister-in-law, but—'

'An event business, isn't it?'

'Weddings. But—'

'An event is an event, isn't it? Is this the same sister who runs the events at your old home?'

Wendy closed her eyes and took a deep breath.

'Yes, it is. She's a wedding planner but she also runs a Christmas ghost tour and fair at the Manor.'

'A Christmas fair?' Graham's eyes lit up.

'She's on her honeymoon, Graham,' said Wendy quickly. 'She can't help. We've got one week and even she, a professional event planner, would struggle with this. I am not contacting her on her honeymoon. She hasn't had a holiday all year because she's been working so hard on her business. I am not asking for her help. She has enough to do.' Wendy gritted her teeth for a moment. 'As do I. I have worked damn hard this year – no, this decade, Graham. I have put everything into this job, everything. I will not be judged for a promotion based on a Christmas fair that the original organiser couldn't be arsed to work on, for whatever reason. This isn't my job. I'm a solicitor and I'm a damn good one. One of your best. Which is why I deserve to be made partner, whether or not this fair goes ahead. Which, by the way, I don't think it should. Cancel the fair. Make a donation to the charities and be done with it.' Wendy sat back, breathing hard, and crossed her arms over her chest to signal the end of the matter.

Graham watched her, his jawline tense.

'You are one of our best, Wendy,' he said steadily. 'You have certainly worked hard since you started here. We have no reason to doubt your skills or your work ethic.'

Something inside Wendy shifted. There was a sudden urge to vomit.

'But we cannot and will not have a year without a Christmas fair. This firm has been holding a charitable Christmas fair for thirty years, Wendy. That tradition is ours and if you become partner, it will become your tradition. If you want to be partner, it *is* your tradition. Right now. Do you want thirty years of tradition to grind to a halt because of you?'

Wendy blinked, her fingertips tingling as she leaned forward.

'Because of you,' she said quietly. 'Because you gave this job to Sue and then didn't check what she was doing.'

Graham's eyes narrowed.

'She volunteered. And she will be dealt with when she returns. We now have one week to pull off a Christmas fair otherwise I'll be in trouble and so will you. Do you understand?' His hands were trembling as he closed her laptop and pushed it back to her. 'Both of us will suffer here.'

'Because you're going to take me down with you,' Wendy murmured, tears springing hot into her eyes.

'Or you could save us both,' Graham told her. 'I'll take your cases from you. You have one week, yes, but you'll have nothing else to do and James will help you. I'll find others to help if you need them, just say. We need this Christmas fair to happen, Wendy, and we need it to be good.'

There wasn't much else to say, there wasn't much else to

do. Wendy left Graham's office fighting back the tears, hiding her trembling fingers. She walked calmly to the toilets where she let the tears fall silently, her body convulsing as the shock of the meeting worked its way through her. Crying done, body calming, she blew her nose, tidied her make-up and ventured back out into the office. She messaged James – she couldn't cope with facing him just yet – and then she hid in a back office with her laptop and a notebook trying to work out how they were going to pull this off with one week to go, until she had to leave to pick her children up from school.

Four

That evening, Wendy sat at her dining table with her laptop and a glass of wine. Her son was in the living room curled up on the sofa in his pyjamas watching online videos. Emma was in her bedroom listening to music that Wendy had asked to be turned down twice already. Wendy was staring at Sue's to do list, surrounded by the notes she'd made that day. She'd researched event planning and just what people expected at Christmas fairs. She'd tried to remember the firm's previous fairs but her memory of them was hazy. The only vivid memories she had was when Oliver had been small, pulling her this way and that at each bright colour and twinkling light while her husband had kept hold of Emma's hand. Her husband had smiled at her, wrapping a warm arm around her waist and suggested they grab something to eat before they headed home. She couldn't for the life of her remember any part of the fair in detail, at least nothing that was useful. There had been food. There had been bright colours and twinkling lights.

James had sent Wendy the meagre list of contacts Sue had graced him with. Wendy had spent the afternoon calling them to find that everyone was booked. She knew that she needed a venue, which tended to be different each year. She needed decorations and stallholders, she needed food and drink, and maybe entertainment. The thing was, all of that was already on the to do list. She hadn't learned anything new. The day had been a waste.

Wendy stared at her blank phone, sipped her wine and then sighed. Picking up the phone, she checked on Oliver, listened out for Emma and, satisfied both children were safe and doing what they should be doing, she called a friend.

'Help,' she said after she'd finished explaining the situation.

There was a pause at the other end of the line.

'Are you sure you want my help?' asked Beth. 'Sounds to me like you should tell your boss where to stick it.'

'Ten years, Beth. Just over ten years I've been working my arse off at this firm and I'm so close. I'm a week away from making partner and all I have to do is put together a Christmas fair.'

'In a week. Less than a week, actually,' Beth pointed out. 'It's on the Friday, right? There's really not a lot of time.'

'Which is why I'm asking you for help. I didn't want to bother Eve on her honeymoon. I thought maybe you'd have some of her contacts?'

Beth sighed down the phone.

'I don't. But I'll figure it out. I'll help but I'm not happy about this and I'll tell you why. I don't mind helping you put on an event at short notice, especially if it's something you really want. But I'm not happy about you being used like this. You know what my experience of this is? You do all the work, you put together the best event possible and you still don't get the promotion. What're you going to do if that happens?'

Wendy clenched her eyes shut. That didn't bear thinking about.

'Trying not to think about that,' she said quietly.

'Is she in trouble?' Something about the deep voice of Wendy's big brother in the background made her insides relax a little.

'Tell you later,' Beth told him. 'I'm in London right now with Glen,' she continued to Wendy. 'I'll see what I can pull together and I'll meet you tomorrow, yeah? Give me a time and place.'

Tears pricked Wendy's eyes. Tears filled with relief instead of the shock of her earlier outburst.

'Thank you so much. I owe you. Big time.'

'Of course you don't. You're family. But if you don't get this promotion, I'm going to punch your boss in his face.'

Wendy laughed. They spoke a little more and then Beth handed the phone to Wendy's brother.

'Why are we punching your boss in the face?' Glen asked.

'Beth will explain, I'm sure,' said Wendy.

'You okay? You sound wobbly.'

'I…Yeah, I'm fine,' said Wendy, her stomach turning as she lied. She wasn't fine. Placing a hand on her belly, she drifted from the conversation. The last time she'd felt this way was the day she'd asked her husband for a divorce.

'…Nice to have two weeks off for once. So we're spending Christmas with Jeff and Eve. Are you coming?'

'I am,' said Wendy. 'The kids are going to their dad's so…' Wendy drifted off as an idea wedged itself into her thoughts.

'Okay. We'll miss them.'

'Yeah.'

'Rob's coming. We gave him the choice this year and he said he wanted to go to the Manor. Pretty sure it's just so he can eat everything Beth bakes.'

'That's nice. I feel like I haven't seen Rob in ages.' It had been a year since Wendy had seen her nephew. She imagined he'd grown another few inches, he'd be a full adult now. She really needed to make more time for family. Her gaze drifted through the doors to the living room where she could still make out the sound of the video Oliver was watching.

They said their goodbyes and Wendy promised to

message Beth of a place to meet the following morning. Once they'd hung up, Wendy called her ex-husband and crossed her toes, hidden in their cosy socks, that he'd agree to have the children a week early.

Beth met Wendy by the Tube station for a quick coffee.

'Feels like a while,' Beth said. 'How are you?'

Wendy's shoulders sank down. She hadn't even realised they were basically in her ears.

'Stressed,' she said with a small laugh.

Beth looked on with concern.

'Glen told me the other day how much you loved Christmas when you were a kid. Even at university, you'd always come home dressed in special Christmas outfits.' Beth smiled. 'Did you come home dressed as a reindeer once? Please tell me that's true.'

Wendy nearly spat out her coffee.

'Oh. I did. I'd forgotten about that.' She grinned. 'Not dressed as an actual reindeer. I had a reindeer patterned dress on but I did walk into the house wearing a pair of these soft antlers. I remember Dad and Jeff laughing. Glen and Mum thought I was mad.' Her grin softened at the memory. 'Glen always was more like Mum.'

Beth cocked her head to the side, studying her.

'Who are you most like?'

Wendy frowned.

'People used to say I was like Dad. Turning up with antlers was something he'd do.' She looked up into Beth's eyes. 'I don't know who I'm like anymore,' she said quietly.

'You're like you,' Beth told her, putting a reassuring hand on hers. 'Don't shout at me but I spoke to Eve.'

'You didn't have to do that,' said Wendy immediately, pulling away.

'Yes I did. You want this fair to go well and the only person with the ability to pull something like this off in a week is Eve. You need her contacts if nothing else. She emailed everything over to me, I've forwarded it to you.'

Wendy hesitated. She really hadn't wanted to disturb her new sister-in-law. Beth had been friends with Eve since they were students and now it looked like Beth was on her way to becoming Wendy's other sister-in-law. They'd become one big family fast, maybe she shouldn't feel so guilty.

'Thank you,' she said. 'So much. Thank you. I really appreciate it. You have no idea how much.'

Beth smiled and drained her coffee.

'No, I do. You forget that I used to work in London, all high and mighty with lots of figures in my salary. I remember the pressure, the stress. What I want you to remember, or to know, is that there are other ways. I mean, look at me. I left all that pressure and stress behind and now I run a successful bakery, I'm working with my best friends, helping with the catering at events and I'm with an incredible man who I love.'

'I won't tell my brother,' said Wendy without missing a beat. They smiled at one another.

'There's another life, Wendy. If you want it. That's all I'm saying. And that I'm here if you need me. And Eve. We both are.' Beth stood and got ready to leave. 'We're just at the end of the phone, whenever.'

The women hugged and went their separate ways. Beth headed back to Glen and a planned day of wandering around festively decorated tourist attractions in the city. Wendy walked to the office where she found James waiting for her.

'We need a venue,' he told her after she explained where she'd been. Had he slept? His hair suggested he hadn't. That pang of guilt resurfaced in Wendy.

'My sister's given me a list of her venue contacts. You take half, I'll take the other. Let's see if anyone has availability.'

The day moved quickly, the weak December sun moving across the office. Slowly, as the evening

29

approached, the office began to empty.

'Don't you need to go get your kids?' James asked after an hour of silence. They'd found empty desks so they could work close to one another, listening as they each called venues to ask about availability.

'They've gone to their dad's early. They were meant to go at the end of the week, for Christmas.'

'Oh,' said James. 'I'm sorry. That this is taking you away from your kids.'

Wendy shrugged uncomfortably.

'It'll be worth it in the end. And it's fine. A week away from them while I'm working isn't a problem. It's Christmas without them that I'm not looking forward to.'

There was a long pause as Wendy stared out of the window, over the city.

'You should go home,' she told James. 'It's getting late. And your kids are probably waiting for you.'

'I hope not,' James laughed. Wendy met his gaze. 'I don't have kids,' he explained. 'In fact, the only thing waiting for me at home is an annoying housemate and his loud girlfriend. Trust me, I'd rather be working.'

Wendy found herself studying James.

'We'll get more done if we work through the evening,' she murmured.

He nodded, eyes back on his screen.

'But only if we stay fuelled. I'll go order us some pizza, yeah?' Wendy suggested.

James looked up, his eyes brightening.

'Perfect.' He sat back and rolled his shirt sleeves up. Wendy tried not to notice, never mind stare, as his bare arms were revealed. James undid the top button on his shirt, revealing a hint of dark hair that possibly covered his chest. Wendy blinked and looked away. 'I'll grab some more coffee,' he added, going to stand.

'Yes,' said Wendy, the word coming too fast. 'I'll go, erm, order that pizza.' She watched him walk away towards the coffee machine. What was going on with her? Her stomach was churning, her heart pounding. She was hungry. It was the hunger and the stress, and maybe too much caffeine. That was all. Finding her phone, she went to order the pizza. Once she had some food inside her and had gotten some work done, everything would settle down.

Five

'That's it,' said James, slamming the phone down and grabbing a slice of pizza. 'It's official. There are no venues available next Friday in London. The city is booked solid.'

Wendy groaned, covering her face with her hands and pulling on her hair in frustration before straightening, composing herself. It was just gone half seven and they'd wasted another day trying to find a venue, any venue, that was available on Friday. Wendy crossed her arms on the desk and lay her head on one arm. It would be so easy to go to sleep.

'Why hadn't Sue done anything?' she said. 'Was she angry? Was she trying to get Graham in trouble?'

James finished his slice of pizza and shrugged.

'I don't know. I haven't been here long enough to really understand the politics of this place.'

Wendy studied him until her neck hurt and she was forced to sit up again.

'How long have you been here?' she asked.

'I guess maybe seven or eight months,' said James, leaning back in his chair and stretching his arms above his head. Wendy yanked her gaze from his arms and chest and back to the papers on her desk.

'You're a little older than the juniors we normally get,'

she said.

'Yeah. I'm one of those people who gets to their late twenties, gets the promotion they've been working for and realises it's not everything they thought it would be. I think they call it a quarter-life crisis, although I had mine a little late.'

'What were you doing? I mean, what was the promotion?'

James grinned and Wendy faltered. Evening James was different to normal working hours James. He had relaxed now that the office was dark and it was just the two of them. Exhaustion and pizza probably helped. The man was not just attractive, he had the most amazing smile. Wendy swallowed, discovered her mouth was dry and sipped at her lukewarm coffee. She pulled a face at the taste.

'Could do with some beers,' James said quietly, watching her. She nodded.

'We can't drink coffee all night.'

'I'll go to the shop down the road.' James stood, stretching again, reaching for his coat and scarf. 'Do you want anything else?'

'Chocolate,' said Wendy without thinking. Heat rushed to her cheeks. James flashed that smile again.

'Won't be long,' he said, sweeping past the desks and striding out of the office. Wendy watched, biting her lower lip. What was she doing? Sure, it had been a long time since she'd been with a man. The last man in her life had been her husband. She was pretty sure the life of a newly divorced woman was supposed to be filled with new acquaintances and rebound sex, but instead Wendy had focused on her career and her children. There wasn't any time for romance, there wasn't any space left in her head.

There was definitely no time or space for an office romance, that would only cause trouble. Wendy pushed all thoughts of James and his rolled up shirt sleeves out of her head and returned to their still unticked to do list.

33

'No venue. Only a few stallholders. But we have three charities and three jobs on the line.' She sighed, which quickly turned into a loud groan, echoing around the empty office.

By the time James returned with six bottles of beer and a large bar of milk chocolate, Wendy had kicked off her shoes and was contemplating opening a window to scream out into the darkness of the evening.

'Did a venue magically appear?' James asked, handing her the chocolate and a beer. She took them gratefully.

'Maybe we could hold it here,' said Wendy. 'How much do I owe you?'

James looked around.

'Could we? And don't worry about it. I'm earning more now than I ever have. Let me treat you to emergency beer and chocolate.'

Wendy smiled and took a swig of the beer. The bubbles swam through her body and she exhaled.

'That's good. Thank you. You never did say what you used to do.'

'Tree surgeon,' said James.

Wendy stared at him, forcing back images of him up a tree with a chainsaw.

'You can get promoted in the world of tree surgeons?'

James nodded, gulping down some beer.

'In this case, the owner of the company decided to retire and offered me the job of managing director.'

'Wow. Nice. It was a big company then?'

'Growing all the time.'

'And you turned it down?' Wendy frowned. Why would someone work so hard for that job and then turn it down?

'No, no. I accepted it. Did it for two years and then realised that something was still missing. Spent another year wondering if the thing that was missing was a family, realised that it was the job that was making me miserable. Spent yet another year trying to figure out what to do next and then went to university, part time at first. Decided it wasn't going quick enough, quit the job, became a full time student, moved back in with my mum and stepdad, took a job at a supermarket, worked my arse off and here I am. Bottom of the rung at a solicitors firm in London. Living the dream.' James lifted his bottle of beer in toast to Wendy.

'Are you enjoying it?' she asked.

'I was,' said James, taking a swig from his bottle. 'Until I thought it would be a good idea to volunteer to help organise the firm's Christmas fair.'

Wendy laughed. James grinned, looking down at the bottle in his hand, fiddling with the label.

'It's hard. Being the oldest in the team. Surrounded by people ten years younger than me who have all this energy and all this ambition. It's hard to compete with them. I thought volunteering for the fair would put me ahead. I don't know what I was thinking.'

'No, it was a good idea,' Wendy told him. 'The bosses have noticed you.'

James raised an eyebrow.

'Maybe not for the right reasons.'

'Why? You haven't done anything wrong here, Sue did. And from the sound of it, there's a chance she'll be out of this place by spring. If Graham has anything to do with it. Or maybe she'll hand in her notice and never come back. Either way, it was a good idea to volunteer. You have to do stuff like that at the beginning. When I was a junior I was always volunteering for projects.'

'Did you ever organise a Christmas fair?'

'No.' Wendy smiled to herself. 'But I wish I could have. I would have loved it. Christmas has always been my favourite time of year.'

James's brow creased.

'Really? I hate Christmas.'

Wendy snapped up, staring at James as silence descended on the office. Those three words hung over their heads.

'But...why?' she breathed.

James gave her a curious look, a small lopsided smile twitching at his lips. He shrugged it all away.

'My dad used to get drunk on Christmas Day, my parents would argue and then, to really rub salt in the wound, my fiancé dumped me on Christmas Eve. For a while there, any sort of Christmas music would make me feel sick.'

Wendy sagged back for a moment and then offered him some of the chocolate.

'I'm not surprised,' she said. 'I think that would probably do it for me too.'

James declined the offer, the dark shadow that had passed over his eyes as he spoke lifting as he looked up at her. His eyes were a delicious shade of dark chocolate in this light and in that moment, Wendy became acutely aware of how alone they were in the office.

'So why do you love Christmas?' he asked.

Wendy took a gulp of beer, giving it some thought.

'The opposite reasons, I guess. Except for the fiancé. My husband never cared much about Christmas. It's just another day. That's what he'd always say. But when I was little, my family was all about Christmas.' Wendy smiled as the memories flooded through. 'My dad was the playful sort. In the last few years of his life, he worked with my new sister-in-law to hold Christmas ghost tours at our old family home without telling any of us. I reckon he knew we'd all disapprove. Mum would have disapproved. She's the one who made that house a home. Christmas was always twinkling lights and hot chocolate with marshmallows, incredible food and amazing smells, and always the biggest tree my dad could find that year. We'd all decorate it together.' Wendy chuckled to herself. 'I'd race with my brothers up the stairs to reach the highest branches but it was always Dad's job to put the angel on top. On their first Christmas together, my mum gave him this angel for the tree with this hilarious look on her face. Like she really didn't appreciate having a tree up her skirt.

Dad loved her.' Wendy softened. 'My little brother puts her on the top of the tree now. I guess that's the difference. A happy family. Sure, there were arguments, there were five of us. But someone always played peacemaker.' Wendy realised she'd been talking for too long and stopped herself, adding quietly, 'Christmas was always magic.' She looked up to find James staring at her, his eyes soft but his brow creased in question.

'Racing up the stairs to decorate the top of the tree?' he asked. 'What sort of house was this?'

Heat rushed to Wendy's chest and cheeks.

'Erm…an old manor house. It's called the Manor, actually. I grew up in a little town about an hour or so from London.'

'You're from money,' James said gently.

Wendy flinched.

'I guess. That's not to say my parents didn't work damn hard though.'

'Oh, I have no doubt,' said James, his voice softening. 'You've got an incredible work ethic.'

Wendy glanced at him to check if he was joking. There was nothing mocking about the look he was giving her.

'Well, it hardly matters. My parents are gone, the money is mostly gone. Dad passed away two years ago, he left the house to my little brother and I spent my inheritance on my divorce. The rest has gone into a fund for my kids when they get old enough.'

'He left the house to the youngest? That's…different,' said James.

'Hmm. Jeff's an architect. He always took after Dad the most. I think that's why.'

'You weren't happy about it?'

Wendy looked up in surprise. What had she done to give that away? She gave him a weak smile.

'I had this stupid notion that moving to my old child-hood home would fix my marriage.'

It was James's turn to sigh.

'Sorry about your marriage.'

'Sorry about your fiancé. That's horrible. What a bitch to do it on Christmas Eve,' said Wendy without thinking. She snapped her mouth closed but James laughed.

'Yeah, turns out she was sleeping with my friend's brother and she wanted to spend Christmas with him.'

Wendy's eyebrows shot up, her mouth hanging open. James waved her shock away.

'It's fine. It was a while ago.'

There was a comfortable pause as they both looked down at their laptops, trying to remember what they were there for.

'Why did you choose to become a solicitor, after all that?' Wendy asked quietly.

When James didn't answer immediately, she glanced up at him. He was looking up at the ceiling, lifting his beer to his lips. After he'd swallowed his mouthful, he flashed a smile at her.

'I wanted to help people. How cheesy is that?'

'Not at all,' said Wendy. 'It's the only good reason to get into it. It's why I got into it. Well, that and the money.'

They stared at one another for a moment and then both burst out laughing.

'Oh, what're we gonna do about this stupid venue?' James groaned, sitting up properly and nudging his laptop. 'Can we do it here? How about an online fair?'

Wendy pulled a face. The beer had seeped into her mind, thoughts crashing into one another.

'Hang on,' she said, pulling out her phone. James watched, leaning forward as if that would help him see what she was typing. 'There.' She hit send and then stared at her phone, waiting for those little dots that suggested Eve was messaging her back.

'What's there? What have you done?' asked James, straining to see.

'Messaged my sister-in-law. She's on her honeymoon but needs must. Now that she's married my little brother, the Manor is also hers. We run a wedding planning business together.' Wendy hiccupped and smacked a hand over her mouth. James gave her an amused grin. 'That's a lie,' she said, removing her hand. 'I'm a silent partner in her events business. Jeff will say no if I ask him, but he can't say no to her. Because he's so in love, blah, blah, blah.'

James raised an eyebrow.

'Don't tell me divorce has made you cynical?'

Wendy laughed.

'Of course it has. Didn't your experience make you cynical?'

James nodded.

'Yeah but if the last few years have taught me anything, it's that love matters. Sex without love is boring.' He smacked his hand over his mouth then, eyes wide, cheeks blushing. Wendy laughed.

'Don't worry,' she told him. 'I won't think any less of you for that.'

'No more drinking when working,' said James.

They clinked their beers together and Wendy's phone beeped.

'Is that your sister?'

Wendy opened the message, her heart pounding, stomach turning. What was she doing?

She read the message and jumped to her feet, pounding the air with her fist and hollering into the dark, empty building. James watched.

'Is that a yes?'

'James. We are officially using the Manor as the venue for this year's Christmas fair. Do you know what that means?' Wendy held out a hand and James took it as a sign to stand up.

'What does it mean?'

'It means that this Christmas fair is going to be the best one this firm has ever held.'

They clinked their beers together again and James drained his as Wendy messaged Eve back.

Six

'What happened after that?'

Wendy sat in Beth's bakery on the high street of the town she grew up in. The windows were steamed up around stickers of snowflakes, soft Christmas music was playing and there was the ever present smell of coffee and sweet treats in the air. Wendy had her elbows on the table in the window of the café, her head in her hands. She groaned loudly.

'Nothing. I think,' she said, her words muffled.

'And you've been working with him since? I mean, you've seen him since, right?' came Beth's voice. Wendy did a strange nod, still not removing her face from her hands.

'So, what's the problem?'

The problem was that the evening alone with James in the office had broken something. There was now something unspoken between them. Words desperate to be said. The following morning, Wendy had walked into the office with a pounding headache and little recollection of getting home. She'd drunk too much coffee and when faced with James, had skipped over the awkward silence he'd introduced and become the most professional solicitor she could be.

With the Manor booked as the venue and Eve eager to help, even from abroad, the fair had pretty much organised itself. Eve had built up such goodwill over the years that the stallholders from the Manor's earlier fair were happy to return at such short notice.

'You like him, don't you,' said Beth, sitting back with a smile like a proud detective who had just solved a case.

Wendy's stomach did a small panicked flutter.

'He's a nice guy,' she tried.

'No. No. I mean you like him. The same way I like your brother.'

'Don't,' Wendy warned.

'You want to kiss him. And sleep next to him. And—'

'Don't!'

Beth beamed at her, the grin slowly fading as Wendy didn't smile back.

'Seriously, what's the problem? He sounds great. And like maybe he feels the same way. You're allowed to be attracted to someone, you know. You're allowed to indulge yourself. Have sex, be reckless, fall in love, have some fun. Whatever you want.'

Wendy's heart pounded, her head spinning.

'I can't.'

'Why not?'

'Because I'm a mother and a solicitor and I want to make partner,' Wendy blurted.

Beth blinked.

'And mothers can't fall in love? Solicitors can't have any fun?'

Wendy struggled, shifting in her chair. Beth leaned across the table and asked in a quiet voice, 'What happens after you make partner? What then?'

Wendy stopped. Holding her breath, she thought furiously. What would happen then?

'Well,' she started slowly. 'I'll be earning more.'

'Yeah. So?' Beth said.

'So, I don't have to worry anymore.'

'You're worrying about money?' Beth asked.

There was the tinkle of the bell over the door and then, 'Why are you worried about money? Do you need help?'

Wendy smiled, turning to look up at her big brother as he entered the café with a concerned frown. Beth smiled and stood, going up on tiptoe to kiss Glen's lips before asking if he wanted a coffee. He nodded and pulled a chair up to their table.

'No. No, I'm not worried about money,' Wendy told them both.

'So is making partner really that important?' Beth asked from the coffee machine.

'What? She's been talking about running a law firm since we were little,' said Glen.

'Do partners actually run the firm?' Beth reappeared with a coffee for Glen and a plate of three freshly baked mince pies. Glen immediately took one and bit into it. He'd always been bigger than their dad and Jeff, he'd always had broader shoulders and thicker muscles. As he'd aged, he started to put weight on but he'd definitely put more on since he and Beth had gotten together. He said eating delicious things was one of the benefits of somehow convincing Beth to fall in love with him.

'That's exactly what it means,' said Wendy.

'So you can't just leave and start your own law firm? The same way I left my job and started a bakery?'

'You could do that,' said Glen before finishing off the mince pie.

'Yeah, but…' Wendy drifted off. She frowned. There were arguments against starting her own law firm, it was just that in that moment, she couldn't think of them.

'That way you could get together with this James guy and it wouldn't matter that you work together or you're more senior than him or that you'd become his boss,' said Beth. 'Because that's the problem, right?'

Wendy stared at her.

'Is it?' She glanced at Glen who shrugged, swallowing

his mouthful.

'Who's James?' he asked.

Wendy turned her attention back to Beth.

'That's not the problem,' she said, although as the words came out something inside her recoiled.

'Then what is?' Beth asked.

A silence descended upon the table as Wendy searched for a reply. Eventually, she shook her head.

'I'm not attracted to him. There is no problem. There.' Wendy took her mince pie and bit defiantly into it. The pastry melted in her mouth and she let out a moan without thinking. Glen smiled knowingly. 'So, the Christmas fair,' Wendy continued as Beth opened her mouth to protest. 'I have to go to the Manor later to start setting everything up. I don't suppose you can help?'

'Of course,' said Beth. She grinned. 'Eve messaged me this morning to make sure I'm helping you. I think she's actually annoyed that she's missing it.'

'She'll be annoyed she's missing out on her honeymoon at this rate,' Wendy murmured.

'I can help too,' said Glen. 'What do we need to do?'

'Great. Thanks. You can check the lights are all still up and set up the sound system with James while Beth helps me with the stalls, maybe?' Wendy didn't know. She was making this up as she went along, but there was only so much help she could ask from Eve.

'Oh. James will be there?' Beth grinned again, taking her mince pie and breaking it in half.

'Yes and I need both of you to behave. Please. Please don't say anything,' Wendy begged.

Beth gave her a look.

'Of course we won't. Will we,' she said to Glen.

'About what?' Glen asked, his eyes full of sincerity.

'See. No need to worry.' Beth handed half of her mince pie to Glen who blew her a kiss before popping it into his mouth.

'Have you been enjoying this at all?' Glen asked as he

chewed. 'You used to love Christmas. I don't mind telling you now, it used to really annoy me when you married and suddenly couldn't do Christmas your way anymore.'

Wendy looked up at her brother.

'I didn't think anyone noticed,' she said quietly. 'I don't think I even noticed until recently.'

Glen frowned and shook his head, swallowing his mouthful.

'We noticed. It was when you were pregnant with Emma and suddenly you were going to a restaurant for Christmas dinner with your in-laws. But you love to cook.'

'I was really sick during that pregnancy,' Wendy murmured, her stomach turning at the memory.

'You always said you were going to call your daughter Holly, or Tinkerbell – remember? It was a bit of a shock when you introduced her as Emma. Then after that you weren't allowed all the decorations. Remember? Just a tree and nothing else.'

Wendy's breath caught, her eyes burning.

'You wouldn't have put up with that when we were kids,' Glen continued. He grinned at a memory. 'Remember that dress you had? The red one with the white fluffy bits?'

'White fluffy bits?' asked Beth.

'The trim,' Wendy told her. 'Like a Santa Claus dress.'

'Oh, I can see you in something like that,' said Beth. 'That would be very you.'

'It was,' Glen agreed. He studied his sister. 'You're running a Christmas fair to get the promotion you deserve,' he told her. 'It's not right, pretty sure it's not legal, and you've worked so hard on it. The least you can do is enjoy it.'

'See? What was I saying?' said Beth, finishing her mince pie. 'It's time you started having fun again. You're free, you're single, you can be you.' Beth brushed the crumbs from her fingers and looked Wendy in the eye. 'Get back to being you.'

Wendy's gaze moved from Beth and her brother, down

to the table and then to her coffee. They weren't wrong. Something inside her had shifted as they'd spoken. Her lips twitched as she remembered that Christmas dress she'd had as a child. It had been her favourite.

Her phone vibrated against the table as it silently rang. Wendy's gaze flicked to the screen.

'It's James,' she said, picking it up.

Beth and Glen exchanged a glance.

'C'mon,' said Wendy. 'You said you wouldn't say anything. He's probably lost. Shall I meet you both there?' She answered the phone to James, standing and moving away from Beth and Glen and their knowing looks.

Seven

Eve and Jeff had decorated the Manor at the beginning of the month and so all of the lights were already in place. They twirled up the trunks of the trees that lined the driveway and in the grand hallway stood a tall, beautifully decorated Christmas tree, reaching up as the staircase curved around it. Just as Wendy remembered from her childhood. Her father's angel was perched on the top, looking as annoyed as ever at having a tree up her skirt. Wendy was just starting to get her head around the tables for the stalls when James finally found the Manor. She waved to him and gestured where he could park, out of the way but still in front of the house. He climbed out of the car, staring up at the building, mouth open. She approached, taking a deep breath.

'Sorry about the directions,' she said. 'Sometimes I forget it can be hard to find this place.'

'It's all right,' said James, still looking up at the house. 'This is where you grew up?'

'Yup.'

'It's huge!' James met her eyes. 'It's amazing.' He looked around her, out to the carefully maintained gardens that wrapped around the house. 'What's over there?'

She turned, following his gaze.

'Erm, the stalls for the fair?'

'No, the trees, past the hedge.'

'Oh, that's the orchard. We've got stalls going up along the drive, on the lawn, in the orchard and into the hall of the house. There'll be some food and drink stalls but we're also offering some of our own, my brother's girlfriend and my father's housekeeper are dealing with all that.'

'Housekeeper? You have a housekeeper?'

'No,' Wendy said slowly. 'My father's housekeeper. Janine. My brother kept her on after my father passed away. She's become part of the family. Jeff gave her the whole of December off as extra paid leave due to the wedding and honeymoon and then Christmas, but word travels fast in these parts and she got wind of what we were doing and has come to help. Thankfully. I don't really know where everything is.'

James whistled through his teeth.

'So, everything's under control? What do you want me to do?'

'My brother's checking on the set up in the orchard for the brass band we've got coming. Could you help him?'

'Sure.'

Wendy led the way across the front of the house to the orchard. She paused by Beth, setting up trestle tables.

'This is Beth, our saviour. My brother's girlfriend. She's the one who got us out of Sue's pickle.'

'As it were,' said Beth with a grin.

'And she makes a mean cake,' Wendy added with a smile. 'She's the creator of all the sweet stuff here today and on the day of the fair. Beth, this is James.' She subtly shot Beth a warning look.

Beth and James shook hands.

'Pleasure to meet you,' said Beth. 'I'd ask for a hand, seeing as how you look strong, but I'm guessing you're off to help the other strong man around here.'

'I'll come back and help you,' Wendy assured her, wandering towards the orchard. James said something to

Beth that made her laugh and then followed.

In the small orchard, Glen was perched precariously on a stepladder, reaching up to hook a cable to one of the P.A. system speakers.

'Glen?'

Glen wobbled as he looked over his shoulder. He gave up on the cable and turned on the stepladder.

'This is James. James, this is my big brother, Glen. James'll help you. Please don't fall off.' Wendy gave the stepladder a look. 'Be careful,' she told Glen, giving him the same meaningful look she'd given Beth.

Leaving the two men discussing cabling strategies, Wendy returned to helping Beth set up the tables.

'Well, he seems lovely,' said Beth in a low voice.

'Hmm.'

'And younger than I imagined. Although I don't know why. You said he was a junior.'

'He's older than I thought he would be,' Wendy told her. 'He had a career change in his late twenties.'

'Ah,' said Beth. 'Been there. Done that. Baked the celebration cake.'

Wendy grinned.

'Is it the age difference?' Beth asked. 'Is that the problem?'

Wendy's grin dropped. This again. She wasn't sure how much more of this she could take.

'No, Beth. There's no problem. Let's just get these tables up.'

The tables were ready along the front of the house when Glen appeared from the gardens, brushing his hands together.

'I just had a lovely chat with James,' said Glen, wandering over and slipping an arm around Beth's waist. Wendy froze.

'Oh god. What did you say? What did he say?' she blurted.

'Don't worry. I just asked him about his job. Did you know he used to be a tree surgeon?' Glen asked. 'You don't forget those skills. Could be very handy having someone like that in the family.' He looked over to the large, old trees that lined the driveway.

'Will you please stop talking like that,' Wendy said a little more harshly than she meant to.

Beth and Glen exchanged a glance and a smile.

'And stop doing that!' Wendy screeched.

Beth and Glen both jumped.

'What?' Glen asked, looking around them.

'That cute look you keep giving each other. That "we know things" look. I'm sick of it.' The words fell out of Wendy at a speed and volume she had no control over. 'We get it, you're in love and happy. And I'm happy that you found each other. And I'm happy that Jeff and Eve found each other. But you know what? Maybe some people just aren't meant to be all lovey-dovey. Maybe some people are meant to be on their own. And maybe some couples should stop rubbing it in everyone's faces. Okay? I'm sick of it. I'm great on my own. I'm doing great. I don't need anyone else and I don't need the two of you giving each other those stupid looks.'

Vision blurred, Wendy stormed away from Beth and Glen before either could reply. She headed into the house, head down, through the hall, straight through the kitchen, out the back door and into the back garden. She didn't slow. Over the lawn, strewn with the last of the season's dead leaves, to the very back where the ground became squelchy and the roses were dormant. In the corner was a swing wide enough for two, tied by old rope to the branches of a large oak tree that had looked over the garden long before it had become a garden. Wendy's father had put the swing there for their mother and all three children had adopted it as their own. Now, Wendy gingerly sat on it, brushing angry tears from her eyes and instinctively giving herself a gentle push to put the swing in motion.

She didn't know how long she sat there, staring into nothing as the fresh memories of Beth and Glen and how she'd been feeling dwindled, pushed aside by older memories of sitting beside her mother on this swing. She could feel the warmth of her mother's arm around her, keeping her steady and safe. Tears dropped down her cheeks. There weren't words for how much she missed her mother so it always came as a gaping, agonising hole in her chest instead. She inhaled sharply, filling her lungs with the chill of December but that didn't take away the pain.

There was a rustle and the sound of footsteps in the mud. Wendy looked up and through her tears saw James making his way across the lawn. Hurriedly, she wiped her eyes dry on her sleeve, wondering how badly her make-up had smeared.

'Hey.' James approached cautiously, studying the swing. 'I can go if you want.'

Wendy sniffed.

'No. It's okay,' she murmured.

'You all right?' he asked, stepping closer.

Wendy nodded. She didn't trust herself to lie out loud.

'How old is that swing? Is it safe?'

Wendy looked up at the ropes.

'My dad made it before Glen was born. For my mum. It feels safe.' She shrugged and then shifted over. The swing lurched to the side until James pulled it level again and carefully sat beside her. They moved the swing back and forth in silence for a moment.

'Do you want to talk about it?' James finally asked, not looking at her.

'I don't know.'

'I know I'm not impartial or unbiased in this.'

Wendy glanced at him.

'Aren't you?'

James turned and met her gaze, his eyes softening.

'No. I like you,' he said bluntly.

A shot of pleasure erupted from Wendy's stomach and spread out to her toes and fingers.

'Oh,' she managed, looking back towards the garden.

'I think we all deserve to be happy,' James continued. 'Whether that's alone or with someone. I get it, you know. That you don't want to be with anyone. You have your kids to think about. And your career. You probably don't have time for a relationship.'

'No,' Wendy murmured. Her eyes ached.

'I mean, that's why things were weird between us this week. Right? We opened up, maybe started becoming friends. But you don't have time for that.'

Wendy turned to him.

'Is that what you think?'

James didn't reply but after a second, he gave her a sideways glance.

'That's not it at all,' Wendy told him. 'I would love for us to be friends.' She looked down at her muddy shoes. 'I could do with more friends. My husband seemed to get all of ours in the divorce.'

'Then why have things been weird?' asked James, his full attention on her.

Wendy sighed and looked up at her childhood home.

'I was unprofessional. I'm trying to make partner and do a good job, and I was supposed to be in charge and instead we got drunk.'

'And did the job,' James pointed out. 'And nothing happened. So what's the problem? No one knows. No one has to know. There's nothing to know.'

Wendy closed her eyes. He was right. She hadn't really done anything wrong, so why was she feeling like this?

'I had fun that night,' she said without opening her eyes.

James shifted his weight and the swing moved in answer.

'And you're not happy about that?'

Something clawed at Wendy. Wasn't that what Beth had pointed out to her? That she needed to have more fun? She used to have so much fun before she'd started acting like such a grown up.

'I think I'm not happy with how much I miss having fun,' she said in a voice barely audible. Still, James heard her.

'So you thought you'd hide away when on the other side of this massive house there's a Christmas fair being set up? I mean, I get that this swing is fun and all, but come on. Have you tasted Beth's mince pies? They're insanely good.'

Wendy laughed. The grin pulled at the tears dried on her cheeks and while it hurt, the twinge of pain was good.

'Come on,' said James. 'Let's get back to work. We've got a Christmas fair to run, you've got a promotion to get and I'm still counting down the days until January.'

'Okay,' agreed Wendy. 'But first we need to figure out how to get up from this swing without one of us falling off.'

Eight

There was still an hour to go before the metaphorical doors to the Christmas fair opened but everything was ready. Wendy wandered slowly down the grand staircase towards the hall, her gaze on her father's angel on top of the tree.

'Miss you, Dad,' she murmured as she passed it. The angel's wonky smile looked back at her. She paused on the step and sighed at the ache in her chest.

'Wow. You look amazing.'

Wendy jumped at the sound of James's voice. He was standing at the foot of the tree, a box of cupcakes in his arms, looking up the stairs at her. As their eyes met, he realised what he'd said and cleared his throat.

'I mean, that's a nice dress.'

Wendy smiled, holding the skirt of the dress out and doing a small swirl on the step.

'I used to have a dress like this when I was little,' she told him, walking down the stairs. 'It was my favourite. Glen reminded me of it. I forgot just how much I used to get into Christmas. So I did some shopping. I can't believe I managed to find a Santa dress like this. Time to get back to the real me, I think,' she added in a murmur.

'It's a good look on you,' said James, ripping his gaze

back up to her eyes as she approached him.

'I thought you hated Christmas? Can't wait until January?' she teased.

'I do and I can't.' James looked down at the box of cupcakes in his arms. 'Although the food isn't bad.'

Wendy laughed.

'That's not even proper Christmas food. I make a mean roast potato.'

The corners of James's lips twitched up and for a moment, they smiled at each other, the lights of the tree twinkling around them. It was spoiled by James's phone ringing. Wendy took the cupcakes from him so he could answer. He made noises, nodded his head, sighed and ran a hand over his face. The longer the conversation went on, the bigger the ball of dread grew in Wendy's stomach.

'What?' she dared to ask as he hung up.

'So, err, turns out the coach company double booked us. They apologise profusely but they can't pick everyone up from London and drive them here.' James turned to look out of the porch and towards the Christmas fair, with stallholders setting up, ready and waiting for guests.

Wendy couldn't breathe. Her dress was too tight, her chest aching. She shoved the box of cupcakes back into James's arms as her hands began to tremble.

'Oh god,' she murmured. 'What're we going to do? Graham's in London. He's expecting a coach. All the partners are.' Her voice climbed higher as she spoke. There was a pause but her brain offered her nothing. Just icy, panicked silence.

'We could…go get them,' James offered in a slow, thoughtful voice. Wendy turned to him, waiting for more. He glanced up at her. 'I don't suppose anyone in this town has a spare minibus or two?'

Wendy's brain kicked back into gear. Turning on her heel, she strode out of the house and into the fair.

'Beth?' she called. A stallholder pointed her in the right direction and she found Beth with her cafe manager and

Eve's events assistant, Pete, setting up their bakery stall in the orchard. Out of breath, Wendy explained the problem. 'Do you know anyone who has a minibus?'

Beth, eyes wide, blinked and looked to Pete who pursed his lips in thought.

'My uncle lives in a village down the road,' he said. 'He runs a coach trip business and has a coach or two. I'm pretty sure he said he was taking this December off. He's getting ready to retire. I've no idea if he's around or not though. Pretty sure he said something about the Bahamas for Christmas.'

Beth and Wendy stared at him.

'How fortuitous,' said Beth.

'Can you call him?' asked Wendy.

Pete nodded and wandered off with his phone.

'I've called some local companies but no one's got anything available,' said James from behind them. Beth took the cupcakes from Wendy before she dropped them.

'Sit down,' Beth ordered, pointing to the chair behind the stall. Wendy did as she was told, her breathing coming fast, her head becoming light.

'All of this work for nothing,' she said under her breath.

'Rubbish,' Beth told her. 'We just need the right vehicles.'

'And people to drive them,' said Wendy. 'There's about a hundred people we need to get here from London.'

'They could get the train?' Glen offered, shrugging as the women turned on him. 'Nice dress, by the way,' he added. 'Just like the one from when we were kids. Where are your antlers?'

Wendy gave a weak smile. Now was really not the time.

'That's not a bad idea,' said James. 'At least some of them could get the train.'

'Think about it,' Wendy told him. 'If we tell them to get the train then we have to admit that the coaches have fallen through.'

'And you'll be proving that you can think on your feet,'

Glen pointed out.

'And it's more environmentally friendly than coaches,' Beth added. 'That has to score points, right?'

'Plus, I bet they'll see the train as an adventure,' James told her. 'It's worth a shot.'

'Mixed news.' Pete returned, sliding his phone back into his pocket. 'My uncle is abroad for Christmas but he does have one coach going spare. Says we can use it but we need someone with the right licence.'

'That's not a problem,' said James. 'I have a licence to drive a coach.'

In silence, they all turned to stare at him.

'What? Why?' Wendy shook her head. 'How many does the coach seat?' she asked Pete.

'About fifty.'

Wendy ran her fingers through her hair and groaned as her mind spun.

'Right.' She turned on James. 'We can pick up the partners and senior associates on the coach, tell everyone else to get the train?'

James quickly thought this through and then gave a singular nod, unlocking his phone.

'Tell me we're getting a refund on the coaches,' said Wendy.

'Definitely.' James flicked through his phone.

'Good. Can we get first class tickets for the people getting the train?'

James looked up and grinned.

'Great idea. Leave it with me.' He turned away and within seconds was holding the phone to his ear.

'Shall I give him a lift to my uncle's when he's done? To get the coach?' Pete offered.

'Please,' said Wendy. 'Thank you. Thank you so much.' She stopped herself from hugging him as she stood, her skirt swishing as she ran to catch up with James.

They might have arrived an hour later than expected,

but eventually James drove the coach full of solicitors up the Manor's driveway. Wendy and Janine, the Manor's housekeeper, were ready to hand each person a glass of mulled wine or orange juice as they stepped off the coach. On the entrance to the fair, Beth and Glen handed out a mince pie each. Music was softly playing throughout the hall and grounds, lights were twinkling from the trees, along the stalls and around the porch of the house. Inside the house, the tall Christmas tree was lit up invitingly.

Kit was one of the first off the coach and she stared up at the house before giving Wendy a giddy squeal.

'This is amazing!' she hissed, taking a glass of mulled wine. 'Better than tinsel at my desk. I love that dress.'

'Thank you,' Wendy hissed back. 'Enjoy.'

Kit did something of a cackle and wandered off towards Beth and Glen, sipping her drink.

Graham stepped off the coach and took a mulled wine from Wendy, looking around and breathing in.

'Well,' he said. 'Impressive.' He gave her a smile before venturing forward with the others towards the scent of freshly baked mince pies.

The feeling of her shoulders easing down from her ears was immense. As the last person stepped off the coach, Wendy caught James's eye behind the wheel. He gave her a wink and she looked away hurriedly. Unable to wrench the grin from her face or control the fizzy warmth in her belly, Wendy made her way back to the house to restock on mulled wine, ready for the rest of the arrivals.

James managed to somehow reverse the coach down the driveway without hitting anything and picked up the remaining guests from the firm at the train station. They arrived soon after, giddy and chatty and already toasting Wendy before she could offer them the wine.

'I bought them champagne along with the first class tickets,' James told her as he climbed down from the coach. 'Hope that was okay.'

'Inspired,' Wendy told him, still smiling.

'Good. So, now we can relax?' James clapped his hands. 'Let's party.'

'You've done amazingly,' Wendy said. 'Go enjoy yourself. Relax.'

'What about you?'

'I'll relax when it's over.'

Nine

As the sun dipped below the horizon, turning the sky and few clouds a dusty pink, the twinkling fairy lights came into their own. Wendy turned on the outside lights properly, illuminating where the fairy lights couldn't reach, and helped the brass band to set up. They were friends of Eve's, playing at her Christmas fair and ghost tour every year, and had jumped at the chance of another gig. As they started playing, something quivered inside Wendy.

This was Christmas.

The brass band, the smell of mince pies, turkey sandwiches and mulled wine, the lights, the sound of happy chatter and laughter.

'I'd say this is a success,' said Graham, appearing behind her as she stepped back to survey what she and James had managed to create. Well, what Eve had managed to create from a distance, but she'd already told Wendy not to mention that.

'Thank you,' she said shortly. 'James deserves a lot of the credit.'

'Hmm. Quick thinking about how to get us all here. And this is a beautiful place. Your childhood home, I guess?'

'Yes.'

'Lovely. I'm impressed that you managed to put all of this together with such short notice.' Graham sipped at his drink. 'I'll be chatting with the partners about who will be promoted soon. We'll probably need some food for that.' Before Wendy could respond, Graham turned away and wandered off towards the food stalls.

Wendy exhaled slowly, her mouth dry. She needed a drink.

Purposefully going in the opposite direction to Graham, she found herself near the brass band and grabbed a glass of champagne from a table full of drinks and mince pies. She sipped at it, half closing her eyes, letting the music take over her thoughts.

'I reckon I can add successfully organising a Christmas fair to my CV.'

Wendy opened her eyes and turned to James, giving him a smile.

'Definitely,' she told him. 'And I'll put in a good word for you with Graham. You've done a brilliant job. Thank you so much for your help.'

'That's okay,' said James. 'It was nice to get to know you.'

One of Wendy's eyebrows twitched up in a playful question and James grinned.

'You know, professionally. As a senior associate.'

'It's good to network,' Wendy agreed and they both laughed, Wendy trying to keep the champagne bubbles from going up her nose.

'That's a good idea,' said James, looking down at her drink. He vanished for a moment and returned with his own glass of champagne.

'So, how come you have a coach driver's licence?' Wendy asked over the sound of the brass band as they started a new song. James pulled a face at the sudden change in tempo and gestured for Wendy to join him a little further away. There was an newly unoccupied bench that Wendy's father had placed in the orchard so he could enjoy the birds in the trees. They sat down and watched the fair around them.

'Would you believe that before I trained as a tree surgeon, I worked as a coach driver?'

'Really?' Wendy gave him a sceptical look.

'I lasted four weeks. I hated it.' James laughed. 'But I got the licence. It means I'm usually the designated driver for big group things.'

Wendy smiled.

'Well, I definitely appreciate it. This would have been a complete failure without you and your coach licence.'

James held up his glass.

'Anytime.'

Wendy clinked her drink against his.

'When will you hear about the promotion?' James asked as they sipped their drinks.

'Graham says they're deciding soon. So, soon? I guess. I don't know.' Wendy looked down at her shoes.

'What's wrong?'

Wendy sighed.

'I don't know. I like being home. Maybe it's the clash between home and work?' she ventured, glancing at James. The low fairy lights accented his features, making his eyes dance and sparkle, his hair shine, the stubble on his chin darker. A breeze moved through the orchard and Wendy automatically leaned closer to James's warmth as a chill snuck through her clothes. The scent of his aftershave, or whatever he was wearing, twisted her stomach pleasurably.

She leaned away.

'Maybe,' he murmured, watching her. 'Or maybe you don't want this promotion.'

Wendy looked at him.

'What? Of course I do. I've worked so hard for it.'

James smiled.

'Been there,' he said. 'Worked hard, got the promotion, found out I hated the job. Done that.'

'Going from tree surgeon, up trees all day, to managing

tree surgeons and a business is very different from becoming a partner at a law firm,' Wendy told him. 'I don't think I'll have the same problem.'

'At a law firm in the centre of London that deals with all sorts of things,' James pointed out. 'That's why I wanted to work with them. I have no idea what area of law I want to work in. I thought this way, I could move around a bit. See what takes my fancy.'

'What are you getting at?'

James shrugged.

'I dunno. Just that this promotion shouldn't be the be-all and end-all. There are other options. Take it from the ex-tree surgeon turned solicitor who has a coach driving licence. Have you even tried anything other than being a solicitor?'

Wendy frowned.

'No. It's what I always wanted. Even in my teens, I did my work experience at the solicitors in town. Property conveyancing,' she added. 'It was okay.'

'And you stuck with it. What's so special about being a solicitor to you?'

Wendy met his gaze.

'I told you. To help people.'

'Good.' James leaned back on the bench, sliding an arm along the wooden back, reaching behind her. 'Just know there are other options.'

Wendy turned away, brow creased in thought.

'You know,' James added. 'Go with this whole you returning to being you thing.' He leaned forward, extracting his arm and downing the last of his champagne. 'Because I really do like you. This real you.' He stood and went to walk away. A flutter of panic went through Wendy.

'What are you doing for Christmas?' she blurted out. Anything to keep him there, by her side. She wouldn't let herself dwell on why that was important.

James turned back.

'Christmas with my mum and stepdad, as usual. Then

probably just watching films. My housemate's away so I'll have the place to myself.'

Wendy bit her lip, allowing herself to think before she said what her mouth was so eager to say.

'We always do a big Boxing Day here,' she told him, looking up to his eyes as he towered over her. 'Not just family. I cook and Beth brings pudding and things. And we sit by the fire and chat and eat. It's nice. You're very welcome to join us.'

James rocked back slightly.

'Oh. Well. That sounds…Thank you.'

'I know it sounds strange but, really, it won't be. My brothers will be there, and Beth and Eve. Janine, who you've already met. Glen's son. The two gardeners my father used to hire. Jeff kept them on too. And probably a couple of other people Jeff and Eve have invited.'

'And you can just invite me without asking them? To their house?'

Wendy grinned.

'Of course. They don't mind as long as I cook.'

'And you make the best roast potatoes,' James murmured. His soft voice slid beneath Wendy's coat and she shivered.

'Think about it,' she said in a voice equally low.

James searched her eyes, smiling, and opened his mouth to speak.

'There you are!' Beth appeared beside him. 'Time to announce how much money we've raised and bring this thing to a close. Come on, both of you.'

Somehow, without Eve's presence and know-how, they'd managed to successful rig up the P.A. system. Wendy and James settled themselves by the microphone. Wendy's heart gave a nervous flutter, her stomach gurgling in rebellion of the champagne. She cleared her throat as James gave her an encouraging smile. Pressing the button, she avoided James's eyes and found her voice.

'Hey there, colleagues,' she said. Her voice echoed around the fair and some of the chatter quietened to listen to her. 'The fair is drawing to a close and it's time to announce just how much money has been raised. First of all, a massive thank you to you. Thank you for coming. I know it's been different this year—'

'Better!' someone shouted.

Wendy grinned and struggled for a moment to remember what she was saying.

'So, thank you for helping to make this fair work. Thank you for coming all this way. And a big thank you to the stallholders, to the band, and to my little brother and his new wife who are currently away on their honeymoon for letting us use their beautiful home. Over now to James, who helped put this fair together and is your designated driver for the evening.'

A cheer went up through the fair. Wendy passed the microphone to James.

'Hey everyone,' said James, a tremble of nerves in his voice. 'It's my pleasure to tell you that we have raised – and this money will be split between the three charities chosen by the firm for this year –' He paused for dramatic effect. 'One thousand, six hundred and fifty-three pounds.' He looked up at Wendy with wide eyes as he read the number from the paper Beth handed him. A loud murmur and some applause sounded through the fair. Grinning, James passed the microphone back to Wendy.

'That's…that's incredible. Thank you all so much,' she said, her voice ringing out. She couldn't be sure but wasn't that more than last year? 'Please enjoy the rest of your evening. We'll be shutting the gates in one hour so get those last minute presents bought, grab the last of the wine and food, and safe journey home. Merry Christmas. See you all in the New Year.'

A cheer went up around the fair and the volume of voices rose as some people scrambled for the drinks tables while others rushed back to buy that thing they'd been putting off.

Beth placed her hand on Wendy's shoulder and squeezed.

'Congratulations,' she murmured, bending to give her a quick hug.

'I'd best get the coach ready to go,' said James.

'But…you were drinking champagne,' Wendy realised, heart pounding in new panic. James waved her away.

'One small glass. It's the only alcohol I've had today. I'm fine. Trust me.'

Wendy smiled, staring into his dark chocolate eyes. She did trust him. How could she not after what they'd managed to create together?

'Wendy.' Graham appeared as James made his exit. Tapping her elbow, Graham gestured for her to follow him. They stopped in a corner, out of the way, and Graham grinned.

'You've raised more money than any of our fairs in the last four years. Congratulations.'

'Wow. Thank you.' Wendy's mouth had gone dry. He hadn't just pulled her over here to tell her what a good job she'd done.

'I've had my meeting with the partners and…' He paused for a beat. 'I'm delighted to offer you the promotion to partner. So, a double congratulations.' Graham beamed. 'You more than deserve it.'

Wendy had been waiting all of her adult life, and some of her childhood, to hear those words. She'd rehearsed this moment so many times, practising humility and enthusiasm. Would she punch the air? Would she cry? Would her chest burst from happiness? She'd been so eager to find out just how she would react to this moment.

The reality was something she had never expected. Her heart didn't pound, her chest didn't want to burst, she didn't feel like punching the air, in fact she hardly moved. She had to remind herself to smile before realising that wasn't enough. She grinned. A grin was more appropriate when accepting the promotion she'd been waiting so long for.

'That's incredible,' she told Graham. 'Thank you so much.'

If any of her struggles showed, he didn't seem to notice. Instead, he grabbed her hand and shook it.

'No, thank you. You saved all our bacon with this fair. You always seem to save our bacon, come to think of it. You're a fantastic solicitor, Wendy. I'll get HR on the paperwork first thing in the New Year but until then, rest assured that you're going into next year as partner. Now, go celebrate. Merry Christmas.'

'Thanks. Merry Christmas, Graham.'

Wendy's hand was still warm from his handshake as Graham wandered off to find one last glass of mulled wine before getting on the coach. She looked down at her hand and then up at the fair around her. Slipping out of the hall and onto the Manor's driveway, she bent her head back to stare up at the stars overhead, hugging herself against the cold.

She hadn't rehearsed for this reaction.

Ten

Wendy was on her feet half way through the knock on the door.

'I'll get it!' she called to whoever was listening. Beth giggled as Wendy walked past until Glen nudged her quiet.

'Do I need to do anything in the kitchen?' Jeff shouted after her.

'Yeah, stay out of it,' Wendy called back. She stopped in the chill of the hall, away from the roaring fire, and straightened her dress, checking her hair and pulling off the soft antlers Glen had bought her. Then, she opened the front door.

James looked up with wide eyes which softened when he saw her. He smiled, and while his eyes danced nervously, his smile was warm.

'Hey,' he murmured. 'Merry Christmas.' He brandished a bottle of wine.

'Hey. Welcome. Come in. I'm so glad you could come.' Wendy stood aside to let him in. 'Here, find a hook for your coat.'

James handed her the wine.

'Thank you,' she said. 'You really didn't need to bring anything.'

'Of course I did,' said James. 'But what do you bring the

family with a professional baker, a couple who own a massive manor house and the person who makes the best roast potatoes? I hope it's okay.'

'It's more than okay,' said Wendy before wondering what on earth that meant and why she couldn't just say something normal. She paused before leading James into the living room. He stopped behind her.

'Everything all right?'

She nodded, taking a deep breath. Turning to face him, she smiled.

'I don't want this to be weird,' she told him. 'I'm really glad you're here,' she added in a quieter voice. Christmas had been difficult without the children, although she'd spoken to them on the day. Jeff, Eve, Beth and Glen had kept her busy but the darkness and chill of the evening and night had become almost painful. Boxing Day was proving better but there had still been something missing. An Emma and Oliver shaped hole. James didn't fill that, as such, but his presence had immediately brought a calmness to the part of her that missed them so much. He wasn't a distraction. This was something else.

James's eyes softened and something inside Wendy softened with them.

'You know what?' he asked gently.

'What?'

'This was the first Christmas in a long time where everything felt all right. I wasn't counting down to January.'

'Really?'

'Yeah. I was counting down to Boxing Day instead.'

Wendy grinned and for a moment, she was certain that James leaned towards her. A loud peel of laughter broke into her thoughts and they moved away from one another.

'Are you ready?' Wendy asked.

James shrugged his shoulders, adjusting his shirt.

'Ready.'

Wendy led James into the living room, the warmth of the fire hitting them both in just the right way. Faces turned to them, all rosy cheeks and happy smiles.

'Everyone,' Wendy declared. 'This is James. Please be nice. James, this is…everyone. Harry and Dave, my father's gardeners. You know Janine. And this is Rob, Glen's son.'

'Good to see you again,' said Glen, standing and slapping James on the back. 'Drink?'

'Please.' James glanced at Wendy. He followed Glen into the kitchen and Wendy followed James.

'Wine? Red? White? Tea? Coffee? Sherry?'

James blinked.

'Erm. What's everyone else drinking?'

Glen blew out his cheeks.

'Beth's on the tea, if that helps?' he offered. 'Beer?'

James chuckled.

'Beer. Thanks.'

Wendy stared at the occupants of the kitchen.

'James, this is my little brother Jeff who owns the house now and who I told not to go into the kitchen. Jeff, this is James.'

'Great to finally meet you.' Jeff and James shook hands. 'And I just came in for one of Beth's cookies.' Jeff held up his hands in surrender. 'She made me.' He pointed at Eve who guiltily waved a cookie at Wendy.

'We're eating soon,' said Wendy.

'I know. That made it more exciting,' said Eve. 'Jeff even provided some theme music while I checked for booby traps.'

There was a silence in the kitchen until Jeff and James both burst out laughing. Wendy rolled her eyes, smiling, before shooing them both out of the way of the oven.

'James, my new sister-in-law Eve.'

'Congratulations on getting married,' James told Jeff and Eve. 'And thanks for letting us use your house for the fair. This place is amazing.'

Jeff and Eve looked lovingly at one another.

'Isn't it,' Eve breathed.

Glen handed James a beer, opening one for himself.

'So, how was your Christmas? Wendy said you don't like Christmas. Has she changed your mind on it yet?' he asked.

James watched Wendy.

'Nearly,' he murmured.

'Taste her roast potatoes and then give her another year. You'll be decorating your desk with tinsel in no time.'

'Yeah, I imagine you'll be changing the rules on Christmas decorations in the office now you're partner, huh?' said James, sipping his beer. He stopped when no one responded. Wendy shuffled her feet, wondering how to word her next sentence. It turned out she needn't have worried, Glen did it for her.

'She didn't tell you? You guys haven't been talking since the fair? Wendy, why didn't you tell him you turned the job offer down?'

'What?' James spluttered.

Slowly, Wendy turned to face him.

'Why didn't you tell me?' James asked, which was a reasonable question seeing as they had been messaging one another since the fair. 'Why did you say no?'

'Time to go!' Eve declared, grabbing another cookie while she thought Wendy was distracted. Jeff hummed softly as Eve led him out of the kitchen. Glen stayed put until Wendy gave him a look.

'Oh. Yeah, best, erm, go see what Beth's up to. Might go find some mistletoe.' He elbowed James playfully and then quickly left.

Alone in the kitchen, James turned his focus on Wendy.

'I'm sorry I didn't mention it. I didn't know how,' she explained. 'I guess I was a bit…embarrassed.'

'Embarrassed? Why?'

'I went on and on about this promotion. I've been going on and on about it all year. Well, all my life, it feels. And then I finally get it, and heaven knows I worked for it, and then I reject it. Sometimes, when I put it that way, it feels like I'm going a bit mad.' She glanced up at him, wondering how he would react.

He watched her, a smile curling up the corners of his lips. He placed his beer on the worktop and stepped closer.

'I know the feeling,' he said eventually, his voice low. 'You're not going mad.'

Her stomach flipped, heart pounding, unable to take her eyes from his.

'You're just becoming more you,' he continued. 'Do you know what you're going to do instead?'

Wendy nodded.

'I was thinking of starting my own firm. It was something Beth said to me. And something you said at the fair, about everything being spread out, helping so many different people in so many different ways. When I was young, I wanted to help the people who couldn't afford the big, shiny London solicitors. So that's what I'm going to do.'

'Some would argue that isn't the best way of making money,' said James.

'Well, maybe I didn't become a solicitor for the money after all.'

They stared at one another for a long time. James stepped closer just as a nagging feeling dawned on Wendy.

'Oh, the potatoes.'

She turned from him and opened the oven. Steam erupted, pushing James away, and Wendy pulled out the tray of roast potatoes and vegetables, giving it a shake and placing it on the hob.

'Wow.' James peered over her shoulder. 'They look good.'

'Told you,' she murmured, turning her head to find him irresistibly close. She caught his eyes and for a moment, she wondered if he would kiss her. Or if she should lean forward and kiss him.

The smoke alarm on the ceiling by the back door began beeping, making both of them jump.

'Damn.' Wendy moved to close the oven as James pounced on the back door to open it. Wendy pointed to the button she didn't have a hope in reaching to turn the alarm off and James pulled over a chair to stand on in order to press it.

'Everything okay?' Jeff appeared at the door. 'You never set the smoke alarm off.'

'Sorry. Sorry, I opened the oven door and forgot to open the back door and…I think we're nearly ready. Go check the table,' said Wendy, surveying the food.

Jeff nodded and left them alone again.

'Have you told Graham yet?' James asked, waving a tea towel at the smoke alarm to stop it from going off again. 'About your new firm dream?'

Wendy nodded, pouring herself a glass of wine.

'I've already handed my notice in.'

'Wow. It's really happening.'

'Yeah.' Wendy sipped her drink.

'Nervous?'

Wendy gave that some thought.

'No, actually.' She grinned at James. 'I mean, a little bit but more excited, I think.'

'That means it's the right thing,' James told her, slowly moving closer. 'How long is your notice?'

'Three months. Enough to get the foundations of the new business up and running.'

'So, in three months we won't be working together anymore.'

Wendy looked up into those dark eyes of his.

'No. We won't.'

Did that mean what she thought it meant? Would working together have stopped them?

'I really do like you, Wendy.'

Wendy, mouth dry and heart pounding, smiled.

'I really like you too.'

James stepped up to her and leaned down. She went up on tiptoe without thinking until their lips met. The kiss was slow, although it probably only lasted seconds. His lips were warm and tangy with the taste of beer. He inhaled as they kissed, breathing her in. She rocked back as they parted, checking the door behind James. No one was there, no one was watching. No one was watching her other than James. His full attention was on her, his eyes soft.

'And there's not even any mistletoe,' she murmured.

James clicked his fingers.

'Knew I'd forgotten something.'

They gazed into one another's eyes for a delicious moment, both smiling until Wendy's thoughts offered her something.

'It's strange,' she said, the back of her mind piecing things together despite her urgent need to kiss James again before anyone walked in. 'Two years ago, my father passed away and weeks later, on the day before Christmas Eve, Jeff and Eve got together. Now they're married. Beth and Glen met that Boxing Day and, you know, I think that's when I realised my marriage was over. Last year, Beth and Glen finally got together on Boxing Day and a month later, I was getting divorced. And now, here we are, Boxing Day and I'm kissing a gorgeous, intelligent man in my father's kitchen.'

James smiled, sliding an arm around her waist. She allowed him to pull her closer.

'You think it's all connected?' he asked.

'Jeff said something weird happened when he and Eve got together. Pictures of Jeff falling off the walls in front of Eve. Like Dad was still here, pushing them together. And Beth and Glen wouldn't have met if they hadn't gotten together.'

'We would still have met. We might even still be kissing right now,' James told her, his thumb stroking her side.

Wendy shook her head.

'I would still be married,' she said quietly, the realisation hitting her like a brick. She put her hand on James, mostly for support. 'Dad knew I was unhappy. He knew. He left me that money for the divorce.' She looked up at the ceiling.

'You think he's still here? Watching over you?' James asked, wrapping his other arm around her in a hug.

'Maybe. Maybe he's making sure we're all happy.' Wendy looked into James's eyes.

'Are you happy?' he asked.

Wendy smiled.

'Do you think this is the magical story of how we got together?' she asked quietly, hoping that he wouldn't hear if he didn't have the answer she wanted.

'Well, I was hoping that Graham introducing us to organise the Christmas fair would be the magical story of how we got together. But I quite like this version too.'

Wendy stared up at him, her eyes widening.

'When Graham introduced us?' she asked.

James nodded.

'Are you kidding? Boss comes over with this beautiful woman, lost in her own thoughts, and tells me to do whatever I can to help her. He barely had to ask.'

Wendy's cheeks burned and she looked away, staring into his chest. He leaned down to catch her eye and pull her gaze back up.

'Wendy, you made me like Christmas. That's big. Even my mum and stepdad noticed yesterday, they kept asking me what had changed. And it's you. You've changed something in me. In only a week, you managed to make me smile throughout Christmas.'

Wendy couldn't stop the grin.

'And you haven't even tasted my roast potatoes yet.'

James laughed and the sound sent a thrill through her.

'Imagine what you'll be doing to me by the summer,' he murmured, leaning down.

'Good things, I hope,' she said, wrapping her arms around his neck.

James sobered for a moment.

'I promise,' he said, their lips almost touching. 'We will always celebrate Christmas however you want. I want you to always be you.'

Wendy pushed forward and kissed him, softly at first, becoming harder as her hands went into his hair. He lifted her, pulling her closer and Wendy smiled into the kiss.

'Really happy you're together and don't want to interrupt, but can we eat yet?' came Beth's voice from the other side of the kitchen door.

James let go of Wendy but she hung on. The kiss broke and they laughed softly.

'Coming,' Wendy called around James, giving him one last kiss before letting him go and turning back to the oven. 'We'll continue this after we've eaten.'

'And every time we go into a kitchen, and whenever the kids are distracted by the TV or something,' James murmured in her ear, kissing her cheek before reaching for the plates.

Wendy grinned as she began to dish up, something inside her melting at the mention of her children. The ache in her chest from missing them joined with a warmth in her gut that was almost that feeling of coming home for Christmas. For the first time in longer than she could remember, she truly relaxed as James bustled beside her and the sounds of her family chatting and laughing filtered through from the next room.

They carried the first platters of food through, leaving the kitchen behind them. Through the kitchen window, out in the darkness of the Boxing Day evening, around the trees and the swing made for two, snowflakes slowly began to fall.

***

Acknowledgements

Thank you to Jeff and Eve Hargreaves.

I had so much fun writing about you in the horribleness that was 2020. You brought light and joy to a dark year. And look at what you started!

Also, a massive thank you to the non-fictional people in my life.
My husband for understanding when I had to disappear upstairs to write after watching Bake Off. My dad for smiling and nodding while I discuss Christmas romance with my mum. And my mum, for sharing with me her passion for romance stories and encouraging me down this route.

Turn the page for a sneak peak
of The Idea Of You.

The Idea

Of You

Coming in 2022.
Pre-order at www.nicebycandlelight.co.uk

One

'*O*h, I don't think we need dessert, do we.'

Sophie's eye twitched. She'd known what she would be ordering for dessert the moment she'd sat down, having already pored over the restaurant's menu earlier that day. As if in slow motion, Catherine turned to look at Sophie. Sophie glared back at her mournful expression. No, there would be no sympathy this time.

'Well,' said Catherine, turning jovially back to the men sitting opposite them. 'No one *needs* dessert but it is a nice thing to have.'

'I wouldn't say no to a coffee,' said Mark.

That was all well and good but Mark was Catherine's date. Sophie stared at her own, willing him to pick up on the waves of rage coming off her. His dark hair was heavily styled, although Sophie would later describe it as "floppy", and his eyes were a stunning blue. He was handsome, she had to give him that, but if being handsome meant saying no to dessert, then Sophie didn't want handsome. What Sophie wanted was caramelised poached pear with two scoops of honey flavoured ice cream. He winked at her, completely missing all of the signs she was giving off, and then waved to the waitress.

'I'd love a coffee,' said Catherine, giving Mark a warm

smile. 'And I think Sophie, you've had a hard day, haven't you? Maybe something sweet?'

Sophie calmed herself and flashed her friend an appreciative smile.

'Oh,' said Steve as the waitress reached them. 'I thought we could have something sweet when we've ditched these two?' He grinned at Sophie and winked at her again. That was two winks in less than a minute which, by all accounts, was far too much winking. Sophie raised an eyebrow.

'Actually, you know, it has been a long and difficult day. I think I'd much rather have the poached pear and honey ice cream,' she told the waitress before anyone could interrupt her, 'and then an early night. Alone,' she added. 'Early start tomorrow.'

Steve gave a brief moan of disappointment and then shrugged it off as Mark and Catherine ordered their coffees.

'Anything for you, sir?' the waitress asked.

Steve shook his head and took out an e-cigarette.

'Not for me. You didn't say you'd had a tough day at the library,' he said to Sophie as the waitress grabbed the empty glasses from the table and made her escape.

'Museum,' said Sophie.

Steve frowned.

'What museum?'

'I work at a museum, not a library.'

'I thought you said it was a library.'

'Nope. I work at the British Museum. I haven't mentioned a library once this whole evening.' Sophie glanced down at the e-cigarette he was tapping on the table. 'Are you leaving us to smoke?' she asked hopefully.

'I thought you said you were a researcher?'

Sophie sighed and dug her fingernails into her palm to stop herself from launching across the table, screeching and smacking him around the head with that damn e-cigarette.

'Yes, I am. At the British Museum.'

'Oh, well, you can see my confusion. They're both boring, aren't they.' Steve laughed, elbowing Mark who gave a loud, fake laugh. Sophie's smile was genuine. Mark was so utterly inoffensive that he couldn't fail to cheer her up, whatever the circumstance.

'They most certainly are not!' Catherine exclaimed. 'I love libraries. The British Library is my favourite place to go in London when it's raining and the British Museum is my second favourite. How can you say they're boring? They're both so full of…history!'

Sophie's smile grew into a grin and she brushed her fingers over Catherine's leg under the table.

'Not to mention,' Catherine added, 'what Sophie does is really interesting. You weren't listening when she told us about her day?'

Taken aback, Steve glanced from Catherine to Sophie and weighed up his options. Looking Sophie up and down, he stood up.

'No, I wasn't.' He pulled out his wallet and placed some notes on the table. 'See you on Sunday, Mark?'

Mark nodded and Steve turned back to Sophie.

'Do you remember what I do?'

'You're an account manager,' she told him. 'Something about insurance. To be fair, I never understand that stuff whether I'm paying attention or not.'

Steve gave a nod and slipped on his coat.

'I guess you don't want to see me again?' he asked.

Sophie blinked. She hadn't been expecting that.

'Well…I…No. No, I don't think so.' She leaned across the table, looking up at him. 'Be honest, did I make you laugh at all?'

Steve shrugged.

'No.'

'No. You didn't make me laugh either. I think that's one of the most important things, don't you?'

'Not really,' said Steve. 'Have a good night.' He patted Mark on the shoulder and left the restaurant as the waitress reappeared with the coffees.

Mark scooped up the money Steve had left.

'I'll give this back to him on Sunday,' he said.

'At least let him buy his own meal,' Catherine objected.

'No. This was my fault. I suggested him for this. I'll buy his food.'

A large bowl of caramelised poached pear with two scoops of honey ice cream appeared in front of Sophie. Eyes wide, she looked up at the waitress and thanked her.

'Why him, though, Mark?' she asked, eyeing up the dessert and trying to judge if she should eat it with a fork or a spoon. The ice cream obviously required a spoon but the pear looked like it would need a fork, if not a knife. She picked up both and began to experiment.

'He's a nice guy,' said Mark. 'When you're talking about football and drinking a pint,' he added quietly.

'No, he is a nice guy. He's just not…He didn't want dessert, Mark. What the hell?' Sophie put a forkful of pear dipped in the melting ice cream into her mouth and closed her eyes. 'This is really good.' Opening her eyes, she smacked Catherine's hand, holding a fork, away from the bowl. Catherine gave a laugh but retreated.

'To be fair, I've never eaten a meal with dessert with him,' said Mark. 'If I had, if I'd known, I'd never have mentioned him. Sorry, Soph.'

'That's okay.'

'He was good looking, though,' Catherine pointed out.

'What does that matter if he doesn't make me laugh and eat dessert?' Sophie eyed up her friend. 'You want to try this?'

'Yes, please.'

'You can have a bite if, and only if, you promise no more blind dates.'

Catherine opened her mouth to object but then her gaze slipped down to the bowl of half-eaten pear and melting ice cream. She glanced at Mark.

'Sounds fair to me. Sophie can find her own man. You

know, like how you found me.' He beamed at Catherine.

'The only problem with that is that Sophie here claims that she, and I quote, "doesn't want a London man", and yet she lives in London. And works in London. And has friends in London.' Catherine gestured to herself. 'So how are you going to find a man in London if you don't want a London man?'

'What's wrong with London men?' Mark asked. 'I'm a Londoner.'

'I don't mean all London men,' said Sophie. 'I mean the suited, booted, rich, no-idea-anything-exists-outside-of-the-M25 men.'

'Oh, yeah, them. I don't like them either.' Mark sipped his coffee.

'Do you agree? No more dates?' Sophie asked.

'Fine. Yes. I promise. No more blind dates.'

'No more setting me up,' said Sophie.

'But—fine. No more blind dates. No more setting you up. Your love life is now officially in your own hands.' Catherine held up her hands and then brushed them together. Sophie pushed her bowl to sit between them and Catherine eagerly dug into the gooey remains.

'You know, I think I'm doing okay on my own,' Sophie told them. 'Aren't I? Good job, nice flat, good friends.'

'Err, I think you'll find that we're great friends,' Mark pointed out.

'Great friends,' Sophie agreed. 'Nice flat, good job, great friends. What more could I ask for?'

'Someone keeping your bed warm?' Catherine offered. 'Sex? Excitement? Someone who makes your heart flutter?' Catherine and Mark exchanged a happy look.

Sophie pretended not to notice.

'Someone who doesn't listen. Someone who leaves a mess. A broken heart.'

Catherine sighed, placing her fork down.

'Not if you find the right someone.'

'Maybe. And that someone isn't a Londoner in a suit

with a fancy job that I don't understand.'

'Maybe he's an artist,' said Catherine dreamily, resting her chin in her hand and her elbows on the table. 'Or a plumber.'

'What's wrong with being a software developer?' asked Mark pointedly. 'And I called the plumber. He's coming tomorrow.'

Catherine rolled her eyes.

'Can we talk about something that isn't my love life?' Sophie asked. 'Like, why you need a plumber?'

'The tap in the en suite has started leaking. Is that the exciting conversation topic you were hoping for?' said Catherine.

Sophie scraped the last of the ice cream into her spoon.

'Yes. Maybe I should ask about Mark's football team next?'

'Oh, I wouldn't. We're not doing very well,' said Mark, pushing his empty coffee cup away.

There was a pause while they each tried to think of a new topic of conversation.

'Can we get the bill, please?' Mark asked the waitress as she passed.

The silence continued as Catherine ran her finger over the melted ice cream at the bottom of the bowl before sucking it clean.

'So, what we're all thinking,' said Sophie carefully, 'is that my non-existent poor excuse of a love life is the most exciting thing happening in our lives right now?'

'To be fair, we've already talked work,' Catherine offered with a shrug.

They paid the bill, following the long held tradition of Sophie trying to pay more for her share and Mark not letting her. They caught a taxi together and dropped Sophie home first. Waving goodbye, Sophie watched the taxi dip back into the London traffic and then made her way to her building's entrance. She started up the stairs and by the time she reached her flat on the first floor, she regretted the pears and ice cream. Letting herself in, she flicked on the lights, locked the door behind her, threw her bag on the sofa and collapsed next to it. She stayed that way for a moment as the pressures to appear social and together fled and she was left wholly with herself. Covering her face with her hands she performed a frustrated, muted scream and then kicked off her shoes. Padding into the kitchen, she pulled a bottle of water from the fridge and sipped it, trying to calm the sugar filling her belly. Her mind ran through the evening and she cursed under her breath as she remembered every stupid thing she'd said to Steve. The date had been doomed from the start and it sounded like it still could have ended up with sex, but Sophie had too much dignity to sleep with a man she wasn't attracted to. Still, it would have been nice to have appeared more intelligent or witty in front of him. She didn't know why.

Sophie pulled her phone from her pocket to check the time and paused. There was a notification on the screen. She had a voicemail message. Sighing, wondering what sort of scam this could be, she dialled the voicemail number and held the phone to her ear for the message.

'Hi Sophie. It's your Uncle Robert. Blast, I hate these things. Erm…could you call me back please, dear? I have a favour to ask. You have my number. Do you have my number? Hang on…'

There was the sound of Robert rustling through papers and then the line went dead. Sophie smiled, lowering the phone. It was too late to call him now, he'd likely be in bed or deep into a good book, knowing her uncle. She'd call him in the morning. Yawning, she took the bottle of water and plonked back onto the sofa, finding the remote behind a cushion.

**

Printed in Great Britain
by Amazon